GLOBAL WARMING

GLOBAL WARMING

WATER BABIES:
THE THIRD BOOK IN
"THE CONCH CONVERSION" TRILOGY

J.N Sadler

Book Ordering Information

Phone Number: 315 288-7939 ext. 1000 or 347-901-4920
Email: info@globalsummithouse.com
Global Summit House
www.globalsummithouse.com

Printed in the United States of America

Contents

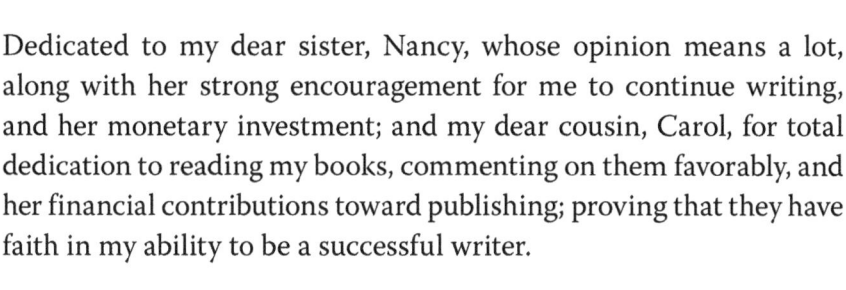

Dedicated to my dear sister, Nancy, whose opinion means a lot, along with her strong encouragement for me to continue writing, and her monetary investment; and my dear cousin, Carol, for total dedication to reading my books, commenting on them favorably, and her financial contributions toward publishing; proving that they have faith in my ability to be a successful writer.

Chapter 1

"Don't tell her!" A woman in a white lab coat warned a younger woman in a black dress.

"You can't let her do this without knowing what is involved."

The younger woman, Dana Blackstone, had fire in her eyes, defending her will to spill the beans to her friend.

"All of this work has been for this one very important purpose, Dana. I know that she is your friend, but it is really not your place to ruin the plan. I wish you didn't know about it. I wish you weren't against it."

She stealthily reached for a scalpel in her bag and approached Dana. Dana never saw it coming, nor did she think she could be stopped from telling her friend of the plan and how she was to play the major role in what science had in mind.

Dr. Keenan Morgan, the female doctor's husband and colleague, came out from behind a curtain that separated the examining room from the changing booth. He clamped a big hand over Dana's mouth. She writhed to get away from his grip, knocking over a lamp on the desk. Shelby, his wife, skillfully and quickly slit Dana's throat, which made her drop to the ground, blood spurting all over the office. He wrapped her body in a sheet and pulled a body bag off the shelf, stuffing the freshly killed young Dana into it.

Shelby began cleaning up the blood from everywhere it had been sprayed. There was slight movement in the bag. Dana wasn't

1

completely dead, but indeed, she was dying, bleeding like a pig inside her plastic tomb. Shelby drew in a big breath, stopping to survey the rest of the red mess that she had missed.

"She had to go," said Shelby. "We cannot have our plan ruined or exposed. Her friends will simply think she went away again on business as she has done many times before."

He opened the door to a dumb waiter. With a few movements, he had the body stuffed inside it, and then he shut the door. It would go to the basement and be disposed of in the Hazmat furnace. No one would question what was in it. He would oversee the operation, just in case.

"The cleaning team will do the detail work as they do every day, without question. They are used to seeing spots of blood in this room where fluids are spilled on a regular basis," said Dr. Shelby, distinguished in her silver bob.

She mopped up the room as best she could, until it appeared as though a murder had not taken place. She threw the lamp into the waste can.

Keenan put his arm around her. "Let's go away this weekend and forget about all of this. Monday will launch step one without Dana's interference. What do you say?"

"What a wonderful idea, Dr. Morgan. We both need to get away. We've worked very hard to get this plan in place. I never liked that little snoop, anyway. I'd like to know how she got to know about our secret. Its exposure would make her famous. Too bad her brain was wasted in literary pursuits and not in the field of science. Oh, here, let's not forget to dispose of her purse. I am sure it has evidence of what she knows in it. I'd like to have a look at her cell phone, before destroying it."

"Come on. It's late. We've got to activate the incinerator before the team arrives. I can get us to our hideaway as soon as we get out of the traffic. We can just put a few things into a bag and we're gone."

They left the examining room and hurried down the fire tower steps to the basement. Shelby watched Keenan open the dumb waiter and pull the heavy bag out and onto the cement floor. Blood had pooled at one end, but remained sealed inside. He turned to the enormous furnace and pushed the button to fire up the flames. In seconds, there was enough fire to devour the carcass of a horse. He asked his wife to help him lift the burden into the oven. She struggled with her end of the bag, and together they hefted it into the flames.

He shut the glass door, and they watched the plastic melt, fold, and burn. The heat drove them back.

"We don't have to stay and watch the whole thing, Shel. Come on. We want to beat the traffic. The team will be here soon."

The furnace turned the bag to ash in minutes, then shut off. "Wipe our fingerprints off everything," she said. They used a nearby rag to do away with the evidence.

Someone turned the lock upstairs and footsteps were heard. a door clanged shut. The Hazmat team was advancing.

"Quick," whispered Keenan. Out the emergency exit in the back. Hurry!"

He grabbed her elbow and escorted her hurriedly out the fire exit, up a stairway into the parking lot.

When two men arrived on the scene at the furnace, one of the uniformed men said to the other, "I guess Joe started without us and left already. He was supposed to take off early for the mountains today. Let's get our load down here and fire up the monster again. It won't take long. It's already hot."

"Okay." He dragged two heavy bags of Hazmat materials down the steps and onto the floor in front of the furnace door.

Nothing but dark ash remained where a dead body had once been. This furnace burned bones and all, leaving no traces of anything. No germs could escape this form of destruction.

"We've had it easy this week with the doctors on vacation. We can get going early, too. Sweep up and stack those cans so that we can split. I'll watch the fire and turn off the jets when it's done."

The shorter of the two men said, "It's really hot down here. I need a soak in my girlfriend's Jacuzzi."

"Open the door, Jack, so we can get some air in here."

Jack walked to the emergency door and opened it, seeing Keenan and Shelby drive away in their Mercedes.

"I guess the Drs. Morgan worked overtime this week and are leaving for their weekend now, too."

The taller one turned off the instant incinerator and left piles of dark ash mixed with the ashes of Dana Blackstone's cremated remains.

Jack locked the basement door, and the two left through the same door that Keenan and Shelby used to exit.

Chapter 2

As Keenan steered the car onto the street towards their lush apartment uptown, Shelby adjusted the air conditioner, so that the air was trained on her sweaty face. She sifted through the items in Dana's purse. Her cell phone would be of interest. She put it aside. They could both go through her emails and texts when they arrived at their mountain house. There was a notebook with extensive notes on their experiment and an article being written to the newspaper.

"Keene, there is enough to bury us in here. I hope no one else knows any of this or has any copies. How did she find out? Do you think she told anyone else? I know she was going to tell Jean, but she wanted to see me first. She would have whether she spoke to me or not, but now, we know she will never tell anyone. We've got to get rid of this and see what's on her phone."

He nodded and drove expertly through the heavy traffic to their apartment over the bridge. It was a high rise with good security and a trustworthy doorman.

"I want you to go into the apartment and pack some things in a small bag. I will wait for you in the garage. I want to confuse Arthur. He's a good man, but a little too newsy. I want him to think that we are not together, in case anyone comes around asking questions."

"Right. I'll go down the back stairs and meet you in the garage."

He let her off on the sidewalk, a block away.

"Keep calm. We'll be fine. Now, hurry. I'll be waiting in the garage, engine running."

She smiled and began walking down the street towards the apartment entranceway as the Mercedes disappeared into the dark interior of the parking garage. Arthur, the doorman smiled when he saw her coming, getting up from his desk to open the door for her.

"Thank you," she said.

"Evening, Doctor. Where's your husband?"

"Well," she began, thinking that he had spoken out of turn asking where Keenan was, "he will be along later, or maybe he will be flying out to Boston tonight. He's not sure yet, but he is not with me now."

She was angry with herself for making up such an outrageous lie. Arthur didn't really care. The night doorman was due any moment to allow him to go home.

"Have a great weekend, Arthur! It's going to be a hot one, I hear."

The elevator came, and Shelby rode up to the tenth floor to their apartment.

Arthur nodded and answered his desk phone.

Now, she had to pack quickly and slip down the back steps. She entered their home and checked phone messages first. There were three. The first one was from her mother. She would call her when she got to the mountain house. The second was from Dr. Houcheck, her boss. No doubt he had information regarding Monday's meeting. Number three was Keenan, telling her to hurry up and to delete all of the messages. Her heart skipped when she remembered why they were on the lam. Disposal of the body was not a problem, but answering questions about where she was on the day of the murder would have to be contrived and rehearsed.

She erased the messages and went into the bedroom to grab items for her valise. Blood was drying on her clothing, under her jacket. She removed the lab coat and looked down at her shoes. Blood had spotted her stockings and speckled her arms. She put the soiled clothing in a plastic bag and headed for the bathroom. The shoes and stockings also were put into the bag. She looked into the mirror and saw there were freckles of blood on her face. Had Arthur noticed? She washed it off with a cold wet washcloth and ran it over her legs. Without wasting any time, she changed her shoes and pulled on slacks and a sweater. Her hair remained un-mussed. A quick swipe of lipstick and eyeliner, and she looked fresh and innocent of crime.

She carried her packed valise, the plastic bag of incriminating bloody clothing, her purse, and Dana's bag with notebook and phone. One quick look around, and she was out the door, locking it behind her. She ran to the end of the hall to the fire tower door. It would lead to the parking deck below. The door banged shut behind her, and she clicked her way down all of the steps to the basement. Her cell phone rang. It was Keenan, impatient for her return to the car.

She answered him. "Give me a minute. I'm in the fire tower on the second floor."

She was out of breath upon reaching the bottom. A fair amount of cars were in the lot. She looked around to see if anyone else was in the garage. Keenan pulled up to her and opened the passenger door. She got in and pulled the door shut. He grinned.

"We are on our way to the hideaway. Good show."

He squeezed her hand.

"Houcheck called. I have to get back to him as soon as we get to the house." She foraged for Dana's phone, in her purse. She came across one that worried her. "She's been talking to Jean. They were best friends. She could have confided in her about the plan."

"Jean might know something, but not everything. She doesn't have the mind to decipher scientific facts or sequences," said Keenan, as he pulled onto the street and turned onto the northern route to the mountains.

"She's been talking to Mark Zabar, too. She works with him at the paper."

"He most likely doesn't know the story. Why would she tell him? It was her big break. I don't think it was more than a 'hello'-type of call. What do the texts say?"

"One to Jean says, 'Sorry I couldn't come to the party. I had a deadline to meet.' Another is to her mother, saying she was busy and couldn't be at the party this weekend. The last one is from Zabar, saying she had a big story and wanted to see him. That one could be damning. He doesn't say where they would meet or what time.

I'm not going to worry about that. The only thing that can happen is that Dana is discovered to be missing. The rest is not our problem. If Zabar or Jean get suspicious, we can go from there in correcting the situation. I better call Houcheck and see if there have been any leaks. That will be our biggest problem."

"Shel, how did Dana know about the plan? Who told her? Did you notice anything funny when she came to visit? Could she have stolen papers or compromised your computer in the office?" He turned onto another route that was carrying them to their second home.

"You know how careful I am. Don't be thinking that I let confidential information go. Maybe someone has been spying on Houcheck. After all, he is the head of the program. We just follow orders."

"We have to go to Jean's wedding. It would be bad not to make an appearance. By then, everyone will have missed Dana. I am sure there will be an investigation as to her whereabouts."

"Don't get ahead of yourself. Relax. Let's go over what we will be discussing Monday at the meeting. I have all of the necessary data we need to document what is to unfold." He opened the window and let cold air into the car.

"It's cold, Keenan. Shut the window." Her hair was blowing around. She patted it in place as the window slid back up.

"I'll mix you a drink when we get there. We need to relax and forget what transpired today. We've gotten away with murder. No one would ever suspect us. The headquarters is not even here. No one would ever find it, anyway. Von Horst is in a remote location."

"We're going to have to make that dreadful trip." She put away Dana's phone.

"I'm not looking forward to our mission, either."

"We will be set for life when we are done. We can get lost in some gorgeous paradise and live free, divorced from the rest of the world."

"I don't want any credit for this discovery. I think Houcheck and Von Horst will face charges, if it goes wrong. I don't want you or me to be part of it. Their desire to make a mark in the world has blinded their fear of criminal consequences."

They rode up a winding driveway to a large mountain house that faced an expansive, blue lake that was rippling in the breeze. It was early autumn. It was still very warm during the day, but night time was cold enough for hearth fires and sweaters.

The Mercedes stopped in front of the main entrance in the circular drive. Keenan stepped out and went around to open Shelby's door. She emerged, carrying the bags.

"Here, give me that bag. I'll put it into the trash in the garage until we bury it up in the woods."

He took the plastic bag from her, went around to the garage door, and opened it, remotely. She continued on to the front door, opened, it, and stepped over the threshold. The air was stale with the cloying smell of dead ash from the last burning in the fireplace. The last time they were there was at the beginning of the summer. They had a lush party for the people they worked with on the project. Of course, Houcheck was there that night.

No one knew who Dana Blackstone was with or who invited her. She was introduced to her by one of the technicians. Although it was curious that she was introduced as a reporter, Shelby guessed that she was escorted by Liam Oster, the head technician. Had it been an oversight on his part, or was it deliberate disobedience of the rules? It was stated in the invitations that only those affiliated with the project would be welcome, but no outsiders were allowed. Everyone else adhered to that rule, except Liam. She was his date, who begged to go with him for the story. All of her notes were gleaned from data dropped from loose tongues of project team members.

Liam mysteriously disappeared that week. Houcheck told the others that he was called home overseas to tend to his ailing mother. No one heard from him after that. His careless move to bring Dana to the party was not looked upon favorably.

Shelby set down her bags and walked to the draped picture window that obscured the view of the lake. She opened them, allowing the glow of sunset on the water spill into the room. She opened the door and inhaled. Leaves were stirring. The world was bright orange and blue. Keenan came up from the basement. She heard the automatic garage door close. He sighed upon entering the room, joining her at the window.

"We've got a lot to discuss and tend to. The first thing is to get back to Houcheck. There are now two people in the project that have been killed. We can't keep killing those that find out. I think we should have Jean and Tom over and see if we can find out if there has been a leak. We also want to assure them that we will be at the wedding and are so happy that they are the perfect couple."

"We were lucky that they hooked up. It makes this part of the plan easy," said Shelby.

"It makes it easier that Tom is in on it, even though he loves Jean very much."

The sun dipped below the horizon, still glowing, sky turning dark purple. Trees were black silhouettes. A cold wind blew the door open, ushering in a bunch of fallen leaves. Keenan turned to his wife and said, "Let's just relax. We can drive into town for dinner later."

Shelby shut the door and joined him on the couch after turning on a table lamp. She put her drink down, laid her head back, and fell asleep. Keenan put down his drink and stared into the cold, dark fireplace. The room chilled. He also nodded off. The room was black around the one light in the room. The two weary doctors slept for a short time.

Shelby woke up first. She yawned, and stretched, and shook her husband's shoulder. He opened his eyes, the whites of which showed in the dark. She smiled.

"I'm hungry...really hungry."

She got up and headed for the bathroom.

"I'm going to change. I won't be long." She turned on another light in the hall.

Keenan got up and stacked four or five hefty sticks of wood in the fireplace and stuffed some kindling around his arrangement. He felt his shabby beard and looked around for the valise containing his toiletries.

He heard the shower running as he passed the bathroom door. In the darkened bedroom, he turned on a small light on the night table and waited on the bed for Shelby. She emerged in a towel, the ends of her short silver hair were wet. She was still beautiful at fifty. She dropped the towel and reached into the valise for a change of clothes. It was her Ninja outfit with black sneakers. He patted her butt and went into the bathroom to shave.

"God, I'm starving!"

"Hurry up, then. Port Pizza sounds good. A few beers and a pepperoni, extra cheese sounds good to me."

She finished combing her hair and applied fresh makeup.

Keenan came out of the bathroom, wiping his face with a towel. He was handsome, hair still dark with no gray, youthful appearance and bright blue eyes. He was almost six feet tall, but looked taller because he was lean. He didn't bother to shower and change. He handed her a jacket, and they went out into the chilly air and got into the car.

Chapter 3

Nara Latimer sat poolside in the afternoon at her desert house in Parchment Prairie. She watched her son, Pisces, swimming, diving, and staying underwater beyond a time that was humanly possible. She smiled and sipped her drink.

"Want some company?" Tom Latimer, her husband, fifteen years her junior, called out, pulling the sliding glass door closed behind him. "I see our boy is strengthening his muscles in the pool." He raised his glass and shouted, "Way to go, champ!"

Pisces did a twist like a dolphin and hoisted himself out onto the concrete. He was tall, dark, and handsome. Soon he would be moving out to live with his bride from New York, Jean. They were both into water studies at college, but she was not a strong swimmer.

He had graduated and was home to visit before the wedding. Nara and his father would be flying out for the wedding in two weeks, then the honeymoon on the Darlington River; the rogue to be specific.

As he walked by his dad, who was sitting on the bench next to his mother, Tom swatted him with a wet towel. Pisces laughed and kept going, calling over his shoulder, "Jean's plane lands tomorrow morning. I want us all to be there on time. You're going to love her!"

He walked to his room to ready for dinner.

Nara wore her black mallet suit. Her hair had dried in the sun and was wavy with light streaks. She looked good for her age, although

Tom maintained his baby face and had the appearance of a much younger man.

"We knew the day would come. Time flew. We have to go back, Nara. We have to go back to Lake Danger and bring Jean back to Von Horst. After the baby is born, they can return and live a normal life. Like you, right?"

"He told me that Jean is pregnant. She won't be laying an egg. She will be giving birth, human-style. It's going to be quite a shock to her when she finds out what's going on."

Tom said, "She will think that the honeymoon was planned as part of her continuing studies."

She stared out into the darkening desert sky as the pool lights automatically went on. Other outside lights went on, one by one, until the area was illuminated. The bright, transparent aqua pool water formed concentric circles and moved with the slight breeze.

Tom became quiet and serious.

"What are you thinking?" asked Tom.

"I used to be excited about my part in the conversion, but now, I am tired and don't want my child or the love of his life involved. It is deceptive, what we are doing to Jean, even though Pisces loves her. I just want a normal life with you," explained Nara.

"I am not with the program at all. I was sucked into this experiment just like Jean. It will be all right, once it is documented. We will all be allowed to live away from the colony. I am sure. We just have to add this last evolved generation, our grandchildren, to our lives."

They both turned and looked into each other's eyes, exhibiting concentrated fear.

Chapter 4

JEAN ANSWERED THE PHONE. IT was Tom.

"Tommy!" she exclaimed. "I'm so glad you called. I was just on my way to a dress fitting. I have to have them let it out just a little bit more. I'm not fat yet, though." She laughed.

"Hey, little girl, you are going to be a mommy soon. Are you ready? Are you sure you want to marry your baby-daddy?"

"Nothing could stop me. Now, I will have everything I ever wanted in my life. Are your parents ready to make the flight out for the ceremony?" she asked.

"Oh, yes. They are psyched. You'll see when you meet them tomorrow. I told them to be on time when your plane arrives. I wish your mother was alive to see it. I would have liked to meet her."

"I know. I know. Well, I believe she is with me and approves of you, whole-heartedly."

"Again, I want you to know that I love you, love you, love you and baby, too."

He looked at his watch. He had a meeting with his parents, and his crewmembers, Ivan, and Jase.

"Until tomorrow. I love you!" She hung up the phone and headed out the door to the bridal shop. Dana was supposed to meet her there to help her decide which veil to wear. She couldn't reach her on her cell, but thought she might be in the shower or had misplaced her cell phone.

The doorbell rang at the desert house. Two men stood on the doorstep. One was Ivan Isaacs, booze-worn old crew mate on the Ocean Glory, and Jason Kinsley, Irish-born captain of the sleek yacht used to explore the Darlington Rogue twenty years before. Although he had written up the report that would have brought the explorers a fortune, Von Horst wanted him to hold off on the paper until the experiment was proven. Tom's hybrid son, Pisces, would provide the necessary combination of human mother and hybrid conch.

Pisces was in on everything. He was part conch, somewhat emotionless or conscious-less when it came to the project. He fell in love with Jean, having her part in the project in mind. She had no clue. It was cruel of him to trap her into a marriage by impregnating her. The honeymoon would be a distressing shock to her, but she was excited about the Darlington River excursion. No crowds, no glitter, just a natural discovery of a new territory, never explored. He had been there only to be hatched. There was no memory of the place in his mind. He was curious and willing to further the cause. Darwin was one of his heroes. He couldn't wait to be the father of the first perfect hybrid human that could breathe in water as well as air.

He looked out the sliding glass doors at his parents, sitting next to each other, watching the glorious sunrise. Before letting the men in, he called his parents into the house to greet the guests. They had all been there, back at Lake Danger on the rogue. They were going to tell their tales about the eddy, the hybrids, his mother's twin that was scheduled for dissection, and his own twin sister, who died shortly after they were hatched. And there were mutant sharks, altered from eating hybrid flesh. All of the failed experiments were tossed into the lake. A smelly fog permeated the little jungle that surrounded Lake Danger. They would soon discover that the overgrowth, the stench, and the shark population had grown.

After throwing on a dressing gown to cover her bathing suit, Nara poured drinks and called to Tom over her shoulder, "When you change out of your trunks, bring the camera back with you. We can reminisce and show Pisces our tedious report we recorded the week he was hatched."

Why didn't you show it to me earlier, when I was little? I don't know anything. Why?"

Pisces sat down with the crew and drank a beer, while they drank Scotch, vodka, and rum on the rocks. He hoped they didn't get drunk and disorderly. He had heard about Ivan and Jase. His dad wasn't that much of a drinker. He had a beer, too. Nara could drink till the cows came home and didn't come undone. Maybe sea snail DNA was resistant to alcohol.

Chapter 5

A CALL CAME IN ABOUT SIX in the morning. It was Jean, calling from the airport in New York, before leaving.

Pisces was already awake and getting ready to pick her up. His parents were still sleeping.

"Tom, are you awake?" She called Pisces Tom. Only his parents called him Pisces. They didn't want to straddle him with an odd name and draw attention to his link with the water. He told her it was his nickname, because he was such a good swimmer.

"I'm ready, and your plane hasn't even taken off yet for Seattle. As soon as the folks get up, we will have quite a drive to the airport. Don't worry. Everything will be fine. You're going to love the house and the pool. It's really hot out here. Don't forget to bring your suit, if you still fit into it. Ha!"

"Very funny. I'll have you know that my wedding dress is still okay, and I don't show at all yet, not that anybody cares these days."

"I do. It's our secret, not theirs."

She ended the conversation, hurriedly.

"I just heard them call my flight number. There will be a layover on the way, so I better go now. Bye, Tommy. See you soon."

"I love you, babe," he said as she hung up.

He ran into his parents' room and knocked on their open door. His dad was snoring. He was on his stomach, face turned to the wall. Nara was sprawled out across the bed on her back, covers kicked off, skimpy nightie opened in the front, exposing her breasts and genitals. She wore no underwear.

Pisces covered is eyes and backed out.

Ah, geez, you're so 'un-mommish', he thought. He guessed it was her wild hybrid streak that made her immodest. He did have time to notice that she had no navel, nor did he. Of course, he had make the observation numerous times before. She tried to cover up more and only swam nude when the lights were out, and the air was cold, at night, or it was just she and Tom.

He closed the door as they roused.

"Let's go! She's in the air. We can have breakfast on the way. It's a long drive to Seattle."

He headed into the living room to stare at the rising sun. The familiar wavy heat lines exuded from the sand and rose to the sky. A quick-footed iguana dashed by and stopped on a rock, nodding its head before darting away across the prairie.

A groggy voice shouted, "I'm on it. Your mom is getting up, too. We won't be long. Good idea about breakfast. It'll save time."

Tom entered the master bathroom and shut the door.

Nara shouted, "They better have some raw seafood for me. I need my protein." She sat up, yawned, and picked out an outfit to wear.

All of the quirks that Pisces was raised with, i.e. being home-schooled, practically living underwater, and eating raw seafood more than most people, would seem strange to Jean. He was glad that they could camouflage most of these odd traits for the scant three days that she was staying. Welcome to my world, he thought and chuckled.

Tom Latimer, his biological father, was the only normal one in the bunch. His mom's first husband was, too, but not her father, Professor Horace Nordic. He was one of the earlier experiments. There was only one picture of him. He had an ugly mug. He was almost side-show material with his white, fattish body and dark polka-dot eyes. He had to cover up quite a bit just to keep his skin away from the sun. He would hide that picture from Jean.

Chapter 6

KEENAN AND SHELBY RETURNED LATE to the cabin. They stayed to have a few beers and watch the young locals do Karaoke. They didn't know the new owner or any of the local patrons. So many people they knew had retired and moved to senior living villages, closer to the city.

The hospital was about fifteen miles from them on the lake. Occasionally, people would seek them out when something of a medical nature occurred, knowing that they were both doctors. Being so busy with the project, which would carry them into retirement, they hadn't had much time to vacation at the cabin. Having no children, they enjoyed company and parties with friends from work. Only those involved in the project were allowed to visit them now, but the reward would be enormous when the finished proof was validated.

They slept soundly until morning. It was Saturday. It was time to call Houcheck. He said in the message that he would not be easy to reach until then. At the counter in the kitchen, Shelby set out coffee and began to get out eggs and bacon for breakfast. Neither one could sleep well.

"I'll call him, then give him to you," said Keenan.

"Okay. I wish this was all over. He will be at the wedding, too."

"So will everyone else. Have you met Tom yet? His family is flying in with him. It will be interesting to meet Nara and Tom. They are the only ones to have traveled the Darlington Rogue River. I wish we could go along when they go back to meet with Von Horst and see the current groupings of hybrid and the forerunners."

"Maybe that is what he called about. Let's be positive. He can't know about Dana. Call him after we eat. Let's get it out of the way o we can enjoy our holiday weekend. After all, we have to meet with the team on Labor Day. I'll have scrambled." He reached for his phone to check the texts and missed calls.

While the bacon sizzled and Shelby flipped the eggs, a car pulled up and parked behind the Mercedes out front. It was a black SUV with dark windows. It was Houcheck and his associate, Rube Rossano, a brilliant, but quiet scientist from Italy. Both of the small-statured men exited the vehicle and knocked on the door.

Keenan slid off the stool and went to open the door. Shelby said, "Should I make more?"

"Wait and see, but it's always a good idea to appease the boss. At least, let's offer them coffee."

He pulled the knotty pine door open and greeted them, extending his hand.

"Dieter, Rube, so nice to see you. How did you know we were here?"

They shook hands and pushed past him into the cabin. Houcheck answered, "You weren't at your apartment, so we thought we would take a ride and see if you were here. I smell bacon. Umm, so kind of you to prepare a meal for us on such short notice."

He grinned. His wrinkled face was composed of a weak chin with sparse whiskers, tired green eyes and a thin-lipped smile. He wore wire-rim glasses and was balding. His hair was grayish white. Rossano was swarthy, young, dark eyes and hair, and flashing white teeth when he smiled. He nodded to both of them. He hadn't mastered the English language, which might have been why he was so quiet most of the time.

"Hello, gentlemen. Please join us. Sit, sit," said Shelby.

She cooked up all of the eggs and bacon that were in the fridge and poured two more cups of coffee, starting a second pot.

Keenan was nervous. "Shelby, is there any orange juice? We could use some juice, too, and where's the toast?"

"It's coming. Hold your horses."

She wheeled around with a pitcher of orange juice, and toast was popping up in the toaster. The men sat in wait of their meal. The butter was on the counter, along with a jar of jam.

Shelby put a plate of toast in front of them. "Eat, while it's hot, folks. More coming, if you like."

She put all of the eggs and bacon on a big platter and set it on the counter. Keenan doled out the eggs and bacon and put the empty plate in the sink. Shelby sat down at the end and picked up her fork. They were quiet while they ate. When finished, she poured more coffee from the second pot. She was exhausted and apprehensive of their boss's early visit. No one ever came un-announced, not even the boss.

"An excellent meal, Shelby. We owe you. Let's talk," said Dieter. He got off the stool and stretched. "It was a long ride up here. I remember the way from the party we attended last year." He moved into the living room and made himself comfortable. Rube joined him.

Shelby started to clear off the counter and scrape the dishes.

"Shelby, leave the dishes. You are needed in here for discussion," Keenan said.

She left the work undone and followed him to the living room, where they took two maple chairs and placed their coffee on the table.

Houcheck cleared his throat. "You know that Nara Latimer's son is marrying in a week. He is the key to the fusion that perfects water-breathing humans. He has chosen a normal, healthy female who knows nothing of what her role is in the plan. He says he will handle it. She is pregnant already.

Rube leaned in. "She will have the baby at the colony at the Darlington laboratory, on Lake Danger. Tests will be done. They will have to stay there for a while before they are released."

Shelby asked, "Can I go along? I'm eager to see the colony and study the specimens. We could be of value at the time of her birth."

"It would be less suspicious for you to keep on working at the office."

Her expression became serious. She was shocked and disappointed.

"Dr. Houcheck, he's my husband. I belong with him. We have both worked hard on this project. Surely you don't want me to be left behind to explain and possibly leak information that is confidential."

He looked down and then quickly stopped. "Very well, Shelby. You have a grain of sense there. We will arrange it. We will need another boat. You and Keenan can ride with Rube and me. I will draw up the plans for your journey. We will make up a mock assignment in another country for you both, where you can't be traced, and distribute it to the laboratory.

"Thank you so much, Dr. Houcheck. You won't be sorry. Rube, it will be a pleasure traveling with you."

"Grazie." He nodded.

She smiled. It wasn't hard to convince Dieter. She thought he secretly coveted her. As for Rube, as little as he was, he was very attractive with his quiet, mysterious smile. She imagined that his Italian mojo could work on her, if he wanted it to. Keenan was glad that they were both going. He wanted to be far away from the missing girl story that would break when Dana was finally deemed missing.

The men got up to leave. Shelby and Keenan escorted them to the door. It was a beautiful, breezy morning. They waved goodbye and went back into the cabin.

As the black vehicle drove away, Keenan said, "That was odd. It worked out well giving them food and treating them like we were psychic or something, knowing they would come this morning. It gives me the chills every time I see Houcheck. He's such a strange little man. I'm glad they are gone."

"Leave the dishes. Let's go rowing on the lake. It's a beautiful day. Come on." Keenan put his arm around her and led her to the closet to get their jackets before going down to the dock.

Chapter 7

Von Horst paced with his hands behind his back in his damp, cave-like office, inland of the lake. There was the oppressive, smelly fog suspended above the silver water, and the ever-cruising sharks were circling in the shallows. What was once pristine water was now infested with the predator hybrid that followed them from Conch Island. Natives that lived on neighboring islands from the colony were transplanted to this new location. They didn't know the language, but feared the scientists and strange cross-breeds, especially Queen Conch. They maintained the primitive buildings and cages and assisted, according to their mental level. The sharks were a constant worry with them, as well as with Von Horst, Barrett, and Moss. The queen's purpose had become obsolete with the passing of Professor Nordic, but she was valuable in the line of descendants that would end with the perfect specimens, mothered by Jean Stark.

The old professor pushed up his glasses and walked to the window that looked out over the sand trap under the automated whirlpool. They had given up using it as a way to maneuver the up and down entrance from the water to the internal beach because of shark activity. They continued to feed them their fleshy waste from failed experiments. Their numbers grew as did their size.

Von Horst's back was pronouncedly more bent as the years passed. He scuttled around like a big mouse, waiting for the moment when the perfect specimen would be born in a human way.

The queen conch glided outside onto the beach to watch the sharks feed. She thought she saw one of the newly hatched infants being bandied about by two or three young sharks in the middle of the lake. She moved forward to get a better look and was snatched up by a fast-moving, larger monster. In a few bites, the queen was gone. The natives, who witnessed this atrocity, ran into the lab, screaming in their primitive tongues. They pointed to the beach. There was no evidence other than a blood-stained section of the lake that was widening in rings.

"No!" shouted Von Horst, running through the room to get to the scene. Moss and Barrett followed him.

"Who got eaten?" asked Moss, panting.

"I'll wager it was Queenie. She saw one of her babies out there getting ready to be chewed to bits." Barrett wasn't terribly alarmed by the recent mishap.

The big-eyed natives settled down, fear on their faces, postures ready to turn tail, but there was no place to escape in this wedge of wilderness.

Von Horst signaled with a dismissive arm for them to go back to their duties. They muttered amongst themselves as they retreated to the darker parts of the cavern.

The three associates huddled, discussing the loss of their prize hybrid conch.

"At least we have photographs of her and data backing up her part in the plan," said Remo Moss.

Barrett chewed on his pipe. "And, we don't need her anymore. We've got Nara and Pisces, and now, Jean."

Von Horst concluded, "We go on, don't we? Another week and we will complete our mission. Then, the world will recognize what we have accomplished. Before they can implement our Darwinian reversal, outlining colonies will already be multiplying and intermingling with humans on land."

"Dr. Wild and Professor Nordic did well by us. I can't wait to see this in a revolutionary documentary. We have saved the world from global warming. Now, all humans will have built-in aqua lungs for effortless swimming and the ability to live under the ocean, indefinitely. When Earth dries up again, they can adapt to the dry land once more, proving Darwin's original theory that man evolved from the sea."

Von Horst grabbed his chest and headed for a chair. Moss and Barrett made sure he was seated, comfortably. The old man had a heart condition that was irreversible and incurable. The excitement was causing ill effects.

"I only want to hang on until the experiment is proven and the world knows what we did to save it." His head hung forward, and he began to slide out of the chair.

Moss beckoned to one of the natives standing by for him to bring Von Horst his pills. This he did, and Moss administered the medication. Barrett helped the old man back into the chair.

"He needs to lie down, Clive." He motioned for the natives to carry Von Horst to his cot in the back room. He was coming to when they hoisted him on their shoulders.

"I'm all right now. I'm…" He passed out again. The natives were frightened.

"Keep going!" shouted Remo. "To the bed, to the bed!" They continued carrying his small body to his room.

"What are we going to do if he dies before this over?" asked Barrett.

"We will finish with the aid of Houcheck and Rossano. I was given word that the Drs. Morgan are coming along, too. We will have plenty of help recording the results. First, we have to get the girl here. I hear she is into water studies, like young Pisces. I hope she feels honored to participate in this research."

"Just for the record, she calls him, 'Tom'." He thought Pisces would raise questions about his origin," said Clive.

"Point taken. Now, let's check the tanks and see about our 'chum' for the sharks. There are two eggs from Queenie and Camelot, the native chieftain, to tend to. I don't know if they are fertilized or not, or if they can be. At least the queen won't be upset as usual when her babies are dissected and tossed away."

They passed through the tunnel to the nursery and lab. Each made a sour face when the stench of putrefied flesh and excrement in the lake water hit their nostrils.

Barrett spoke over his shoulder to Moss, "We have got to do something about the lake before Houcheck and the others arrive. We don't have much time."

"I thought I saw one of those nasty sharks on the beach yesterday, through the fog. It looked like it was coming ashore to forage for food. It seemed to have muscular front legs and webbed feet, as well as fins. Do you suppose..."

"We're cooked suckers if they start walking and climbing, and emerging from water to land. It's the exact opposite of what we are trying to do to humans. Ironic, isn't it?" Barrett pushed through a curtained doorway.

"We need help. I don't think Von Horst is in a position to execute any solutions to this problem. He only sees one thing...the project. We could blow them up with explosives, I suppose. Maybe that would get rid of them. I will ask if headquarters can drop some by drone. I should ask Houcheck, directly."

"Do it now Moss! I'm going to catch up with today's rounds. We will talk later."

They parted company. Moss went on to his tiny space in a small supply room that had a phone. He called Houcheck and left word that they needed explosives and why. The sharks were swimming around the perimeter of the large lake, their fins cutting through mist like shining, silver knives.

Chapter 8

JEAN MANAGED TO CATCH SOME sleep on the first leg of the flight, although intermittent dreams caused her a disturbed nap. As happy as she was about marrying the man of her dreams, she was naive in the ways of love and romance. He was her first real relationship. He was irresistible: so smart, handsome, talented, and unlike any other she had ever met. Their interests were similar. Both were intrigued by water and its properties. Marine and inland waters were her choice of study.

It was exciting to picture herself on a discovery mission: a honeymoon on the Darlington rogue branch. It was meant to be, as the moon was just right. Tom, Jr. knew the way. And, she was going to have his child. What more could she ask, other than her parents be at her wedding.

Arlen Stark, her father, was a retired astrophysicist. Now, being very old and a widower, he resided in a home for Alzheimer's patients in upstate New York. He didn't even recognize his daughter anymore. She visited him less and less. Accepting this fact about him, she simply waited for the time when funeral arrangements would be necessary. She came from a long line of only children. There was no family left to rely on. Tom was an only child, also. It was her hope to have lots of children and build a strong family unit. She was thrilled being pregnant right away. It was a good sign that she was fertile.

The plane was landing at the stopover airport. She didn't have to leave the plane, so she just looked out the window at the other planes on the ground. Before the attendants took a break, she picked up a carton of cranberry juice from the tray and a pack of saltines. She wanted to stave off her nausea. Would she vomit when exchanging vows at the altar? She chuckled inside. Even though she was dead tired most of the time and sickened when the smell of cigar smoke or bacon assaulted her olfactory sense, she was joyous inside, imagining the first time she would see her beautiful baby's face. Tom would be the perfect dad. He had a good future in science, and she would join him in research when the child was old enough to be left with a nanny. She shut her eyes, trying to imagine what the desert house was like. Would his mother and father accept her into their lives as a cherished daughter-in-law?

After a hearty breakfast at a diner on the way to the airport, the Latimer family traveled along isolated desert roads that led to busier highways that led to their destination. Pisces was keyed up over the initial meeting between his mother and father, and his beloved. They seemed delighted that she was pregnant already. What other people thought was nobody's business. Of course, the three of them knew the importance of her unborn child. The sex was unknown. Its conception was not calculated, one way or the other.

Tom went through the gates of the small airport and parked in an underground lot. They were early. The incoming flight chart indicated that the plane would be earlier than usual. This was good. Pisces managed to get his family on schedule in the real world. So far, his life at home was insular. Only in college did he discover life after home school. He was liked and accepted; however, the swim team wondered why he had no belly button. His child would have one and be spared the teasing. Of course, his explanation for this phenomenon was that he had a gross 'outie' that needed re-construction. The plastic surgeon decided to eliminate it altogether, because it would aid his speed in the water to have a smooth abdomen, and it wasn't needed anyway. It was one less place to collect lint.

Jean thought it odd, but she loved him anyway. That was a minor item. At least, it wasn't inherited.

She put her hands on her small protuberance, wondering what it would feel like when she felt life. Dana, her friend, told her that women called it "the quickening". She belched. The juice was too acidic. Nibbling on the crackers settled her stomach. It was hot in the cabin of the plane. She began to feel like she was choking. The air was heavy and cloying. As fast as she could muster, she headed for the rest room to upchuck in the toilet. She hoped that this didn't ruin her visit. She pictured throwing up in the lap of his mother or into his father's face while saying, "It's a pleasure meeting…"

It was short hop to her final destination in Seattle. She was stable now that half the day was over. When the plane landed, she waited for others to file out with their overhead bags, and then she stood up, hauling her heavy carry-on. She popped a mint before exiting the plane and entering the section where Tom and his family were waiting.

She saw him wildly waving, right away. He pushed against the heavy cord that kept passengers from waiting family and friends.

"Jean!" The attendant unhooked the rope and let the passengers out into the lobby. She was not in the front grouping that moved to find their receivers. Tom and Nara stayed back, wishing to greet her where there was more room and less noise.

"Tommy!" She lifted her bag up in a greeting. When it was her turn to go through the gate, he took her bag and gave her a big hug and kiss. She was overwhelmed.

There were a lot of trees on the perimeter of the airport. She expected desert sand, but she would discover that not far away was the prairie, Parchment Prairie, to be exact.

He put his arm around her and led her to his smiling mother and father. Nara reached out and hugged her. "Jean, I'm so happy you are here." She kissed her on the cheek, leaving lipstick on her face. She took a long look at her. Jean was a pretty girl, on the quiet side, but this wasn't the time for conversation.

Tom, who looked just like his son, Pisces, only taller, came forward and hugged her as well. "Jean, you are everything Pisces said you were. Come on, let's get your luggage and get out of here. We want to take you home."

Those words sounded so warm and fuzzy to her. "Home," So far, she felt totally accepted. They knew about the pregnancy, so that wasn't something she had to worry about...no hiding it. She guessed that 'Pisces' was their nickname for Tommy because he was such a water person.

The ride was a long one. Although the vehicle was roomy and air-conditioned, Jean fought claustrophobia. She managed to maintain it until the house came into view. They traveled through a western gate that led to the property. The pool glistened in the hot sun. They had gotten her a floating chair, knowing that she didn't like to swim. She put on her sun glasses.

Pablo, the handy man, was pruning a few green bushes along the front of the house. He was in half shade, half sun. Images were brilliant in this light. The sky seemed endless until the wall of lavender mountains and dark green pines back-dropped the expanse of flat, sandy land.

They got out and entered the cool interior.

"This is a lovely place. It's so private and natural," said Jean. She was astounded at such wealth. Pisces had told her about his mother's fortune, inherited from her famous first husband, pilot Buck Martin. She saw the hangars that held Buck's flying machines, off in the distance.

They settled into the living room.

"Sit, sit, Jean," said Nara. You must be tired from your journey. I'll get you a drink of ice water."

Jean sat down on the printed sofa and sank into the comfort of lush cushions. She put her head back for a moment before sitting up straight. Pisces sat next to her, holding her hand. They were like two teenagers.

Tom smiled and took a seat opposite them. "Do you like seafood? Believe it or not, we have the best. It's imported. Nara is a real shellfish hound. She's prepared lobster and crab for lunch. Of course, we have anything you want, if you don't like seafood."

"No, actually, I love it! It's one of the few things that I can eat without getting sick."

"I know that you have to watch what you eat and drink, so we won't offer caffeine or alcohol, or..."

"Don't worry about me, Mr. Latimer. I appreciate your concerns, though. Our baby will be healthy and able, I promise you. I feel it. Things are good."

Nara entered the room with a dish of canapes and a glass of ice water for Jean.

"I do have an appetite for two. This is new for me. Usually, I eat to stay alive, not live to eat. This looks wonderful, Nara. Thank you."

"I just couldn't be happier to have you here with us. I want you to feel that this is your home, too. I'll show you around after we have lunch."

They were all in an alpha state of mind.

Later, after the group had dined at a restaurant in town, they sat by the pool. The water was still warm, and the lights were on. It was a magical scene. Pisces showed off by staying underwater for an outrageous amount of time. Nara joined him. They both did underwater acrobatics that wowed Jean.

"Do you have the same abilities as Nara and Pisces? That's what you call him, isn't it?"

"Tom is really his middle name, and no, I don't have circus sideshow talent. I couldn't believe Nara's ability when I first experienced it. You'll get used to it. It's just the way they are."

Jean watched the mother and son water tricks, noticing that Nara had no navel, either. Her rambling thoughts stopped short. How could that be? Should she ask Pisces about it, or keep quiet? She thought it odd, but not essential to find out why.

Dana hadn't called. She didn't show up at the bridal gown fitting, nor did she go with her to the airport. It was a fleeting thought, although it did nag at her.

The sky became very dark. There was no moon that night, just the stars that peeked out behind a thin cloud cover. Tom looked at his watch and called out to his wife, "Hey, it's getting late. Let's go in for night cap. I'm sure Jean and Pisces are ready to turn in. It's been a big day."

Nara pulled herself out of the water and wrapped her cover up around her. She sighed. Jean thought it strange that she wasn't out of breath from her long submergence in the pool. Pisces did his special dolphin twist out of the water and onto the cement, splashing everyone in his wake. He landed on his feet, laughing, not out of breath at all. She was glad that his father was normal, otherwise, she would have been outnumbered. She really didn't want to go into the water, whether or not they had bought her a flotation device. They didn't want to see how mad she would get if she fell in. She was phobic about it.

Jean yawned and stood up. She was shivering from the chill, desert night air. Pisces dried himself off with a big towel and approached her with dripping dark hair. He put his cold, wet arm around her and pulled her to his chlorine-smelling skin. She pushed away. "You're getting me all wet, Tom, I mean Pisces." She laughed. "I'm cold enough as is."

"Sorry, baby. Here, let's get you all nice and dry." He roughed her up with his damp towel. She pushed him away, face distorted in anger.

"I said stop it!" Her tone was serious. This was something new from her. Maybe it was due to her hormones from the pregnancy.

"Okay, okay. I'm sorry. Come on. Let's go in and get changed for bed." He took her hand and led her through the glass doors to the living room, where Tom and Dana had gone. The air conditioner was on, but the temperature was just right, having adjusted automatically on the energy-saver mode.

As they walked through the hallway to their bedroom, Nara called out to them, "Do you want anything to eat or drink? Dad and I are having some wine...maybe some cheese and crackers."

"No, thanks, Nara," answered Jean as she continued down the hallway. "I'm just going to go straight to bed."

"Call me 'Mom'," she said. "After all, you are going to be my daughter-in-law. I always wanted a daughter." Nara smiled.

"Okay, Mom," she said. "I'm glad to be your daughter. Thanks."

She went into the room where Pisces was raised. It had some juvenile decorations on the walls, like Aqua Man and scenes from Jaws. He had gotten a king size water bed instead of the child's single that he had while he was growing up.

She sat down on the edge of the bedframe and felt the motion of the water trapped in the mattress. "I hope I don't get seasick tonight."

She felt the swells rolling under her hands. There was a tightening in her throat.

"Once you roll into it, you'll be fine. Besides, I will be with you, even if you just want to sleep." He jumped on the bed and caused an internal squall within the miniature sea's confines. She fell onto the bed and rolled towards him, her body rolling with the motion of the mattress.

She struggled to sit up. "I guess I'm on my own with this. I mean it, I might get sick." She stood up and reached for her suitcase, jerking open the zipper to retrieve her nightgown, but sitting back down on the bed, instead.

He consoled her. The water made a lapping noise when he sat up. She hoped she wouldn't hear the noise every time she turned over. As she got back into bed, she chalked up her anger to the fact that she was pregnant, over-tired, and under the pressure of meeting her future husband's parents. Plus, her brain was working overtime on getting used to calling him Pisces, instead of Tom. Then, she discovered that his mother had no navel, either, and that both of them could hold their breath indefinitely under water. Lastly, she wondered why their breathing wasn't affected at all when they emerged back into the air. She rubbed her eyes.

"I'm so tired." She rolled to the middle. The motion of the water under her actually rocked her to sleep.

Pisces shut out the light and pulled up the sheet, letting her sleep in her clothes, only removing her shoes. He went back out into the living room to talk to his parents.

He found them sitting on the couch, sipping wine.

"I could use a drink." He headed for the bar and poured himself a Scotch and water with ice. He sighed, bags under his eyes. The rigors of the day left him very tired.

"She's a doll. Your baby is going to be beautiful." Nara raised her glass to him. "Cheers! What are the names you've picked…and it can't be Tom, Pisces, or Nara."

"Whatever Jean wants is what it will be, Mother. That's her territory. I wish that she knew what was going to happen and why we're going down the Darlington to the colony to our honeymoon."

He sipped his drink and stood next to the fireplace with one arm draped over the mantel.

"She's a lucky girl, Pisces. You are a stunning specimen of Man." She sipped more wine and looked at Tom. "What do you think of all this, Tom?"

"I wish we were well beyond where we are now. I don't look forward to Jean's reaction to her role in this. She doesn't know anything. I don't like keeping secrets. Maybe it's a human thing. She's so innocent."

Chapter 9

J EAN CHECKED HER TEXTS BEFORE turning in. Dana had not answered any of her calls or texts. It had been three days since she had heard from her. She was stood up twice. Something was wrong. She texted Mark Zabar, Dana's friend at the paper where she worked. There was no answer there, so she left a text. She asked him to meet her at the airport. She wished that the Latimers would be accompanying her home. It was only a few days until the wedding, after she arrived home. She had so much to do, and Dana was supposed to be helping her with it all.

Pisces and she slept soundly until morning. The rooster did crow at six sharp, and the hens began clucking loudly as they ran in circles, away from the trumpeting cock.

Time passed quickly until Jean had to return and prepare for the wedding. Dana's sister, Ann, answered her phone and said she hadn't seen or heard from Dana for a few days. It was highly unlike her to be so irresponsible. She would scout around and see if she could find out more information about Dana's whereabouts.

Shelby let Micklos into the cabin. He was from the Ukraine. His forte was kidnapping and sleuthing. Rossano discovered him when covering up one of his Italian projects. Micklos did seamless work. He was big and bald, about forty, meaty hands, and big feet. He never grinned. Everything was very serious to him. Once, he laughed when

Houcheck tripped over a loose shoelace and fell into a table, knocking it to the ground. Papers went flying as Micklos held his sides, laughing loudly.

He was chosen to watch Jean when they reached the colony on the rogue. He was clumsy with words and not the nicest person to be around, but he was good at what he was asked to do; as long as he had nothing to do with the baby.

She offered him a beer and called Keenan out from the back bedroom. He offered his hand to Micklos. "Long time, my friend. How've you been?"

"Good. Good." He shook hands and answered him, straight-faced.

"The wedding is tomorrow. I want you to keep an eye on the bride to be. Don't let her escape for any reason. We don't expect trouble, but you know the drill."

He nodded.

"Did you take care of Mark Zabar?"

He nodded again, without explaining what he had done.

"Well, what happened? Is he dead?"

Keenan listened intently to his wife's interrogation.

"In a trunk at the bottom of the deep blue sea." Micklos nodded and wrung his hands. He motioned that he had choked him to death, first.

"Did anyone see you at the dock?" He shook his head.

"I sunk the boat and swam back to shore. It was night time. No one was tending the slips. It will look like a joy ride that sunk."

"Good. Good, Micklos. Have another beer. Relax," said Keenan.

Shelby said to Keenan, "I wonder where Jean thinks her best friend is. I hope the wedding goes off smoothly anyway. I guess she is upset."

"She will have to get over it. Right after the wedding, next day, they take off for Parchment Prairie again. We will take the next flight. I understand that the original crew is going with them to navigate. Tom and Nara ae staying behind. Von Horst's orders. He is nervous about so many people converging on their secret colony." Keenan poured himself a drink.

"Last I heard, from Houcheck, they ordered explosives to clean out the lake. It has become stagnant. I don't think Von Horst is too well. He has a very bad heart. I forgot how old he was. Make me one, too, would you?"

Keenan sat down across from Micklos. "Did you find any evidence in Mark's apartment?"

Micklos sucked on his beer, then spoke. "I did find a notebook with the beginnings of a story that Dana was going to disclose to him. I have it with me in the van. I also got his phone and any other papers that he was working on. I left no fingerprints, and no one saw me. I disconnected the security alarm before entering and hooked it back up when I left. This also deactivated the video camera, so no one could see me enter or leave. I even set the time different, so that it looked like the theft took place later than it did."

"Nice work. Na Zdorovie." Keenan raised his glass to Micklos. He sloshed down more beer, and Shelby toasted with her glass.

Shelby said, "Bring in the evidence. We have to destroy it after looking it over. There can be no leaks. Soon, the legend of the Rogue River will be splattered on the news as having reappeared during the full moon this month. Luckily, all attempts to find it, much less navigate to Lake Danger, have failed. Most people think it is a myth."

"I hope no one takes exception to the odds and tries again. We will be seeking passage through the rogue's circular gate at the appropriate time. There will be two boats – the Ocean Glory, the one that holds the honeymoon crew, and our boat, Catfish, not equal to the Ocean Glory, but good enough to get through, following closely. We will have you, Micklos, Houcheck, Rossano, and of course, Shelby and myself," said Keenan.

"I'm psyched! I've always wanted to dispel the myth and turn it into a reality. To science!" cheered Shelby, and they toasted again.

Micklos went outside to get the evidence out of his vehicle.

The doctors went over the information from Zabor's apartment. Sure enough, he had the beginnings of her story that would crack the project wide open, had it been turned in. They would destroy the evidence and his cell phone, after gleaning all the phone numbers and pertinent calls listed on it.

"I wonder how far this scuttlebutt has gotten," mused Shelby.

"I think we squelched it. It won't surface until we are long gone up the river." Keenan stood and stretched.

Ann, Dana's sister, texted Jean while she was on the plane, on her way home. She told her that no one had seen Dana, and that Mark Zabor was missing, too. She asked if Dana and Mark were having an affair. That would explain them both being gone.

Jean texted back, "I saw Mark before I left for Seattle. He never mentioned Dana, other than to say he couldn't reach her by phone or text. He said that maybe she was working undercover on her breaking story. He wasn't sure what it was about. She was supposed to meet him to go over details before unleashing it to the editor. It sounded big, he said, but she never showed."

The wedding was beautiful and private, in spite of Dana's absence. Ann took over and served as her maid of honor in a small chapel outside the city limits. There were just a few people there, including Keenan and Shelby. Jean skyped her father at the rest home, during the ceremony, and even though he didn't know what was going on, she paid tribute to him and her deceased mother for the wonderful love and security they had given her. There were tears in her eyes. The Latimers were very supportive. A modest reception followed at a nearby restaurant in the woods.

There was no need to cast suspicion on Dr. Houcheck and Rube Rossano by having them attend, so they weren't present. Excitement was building for the honeymoon excursion. Preparations were being made behind the scenes at the marina on the West Coast. The second boat, Catfish, carrying the scientific crew, would trail a good distance behind, once they got underway. The crew of The Ocean Glory had been briefed and was waiting for the return of the Latimers.

Chapter 10

Ivan looked awful, like he was hungover and possibly very ill. He was emaciated and showed his age. Jason was his merry self, red nose, bright blue eyes and Irish ruddiness to his skin. He was dressed nicely in clean white and khaki, looking like the eager adventurer. His red beard was well-trimmed. He was ready to go aboard The Ocean Glory once again, as captain. Ivan had lines in his face from drinking and hallucinating that he was onto something big. The reports of their trip to the new colony and the discovery of the rogue had been confiscated from him, by Tom. They were never turned in, once they found out that the experiment wasn't over. The thick volumes of maps, data, and photos were locked away in his safe in the desert house.

Nara was thrilled that she was going to have a grandchild. Tom was glad that it would be over soon. He didn't have a feel for any of this and although he loved Pisces, he felt that his whole life was being a subject to Wild's preposterous genetic mutation theory. He wanted to simply live out his life with Nara, enjoying nature and her company.

The four of them sat around the dining room table in the sun-filled room. a big pot of lobster boiled on the stove, and a large platter of boiled clams and mussels was the centerpiece. Beer and hard drinks were served. Ivan emptied his flask before accepting what they had to offer him. Jase was a Jack Daniels man. He drank straight shots. This was an occasion, after all. Nara drank clam juice, and Tom had his usual Corona beer. She served up all kinds of fish dishes with artisan bread for her guests. She hadn't aged in all the time spent raising and teaching Pisces. Tom was finding gray hairs, but remained a muscular, attractive man.

"So," said Tom, chewing bread and clams, "we leave in five days."

Ivan lay on the couch, out cold. The three companions stood back, looking at him in dismay.

"We have to stop his drinking. He can't go on our trip in this condition. Why didn't you tell me about this, Jason? I thought you were in close communication. Last I saw you, you were living with him." Tom was looking for someone to blame. He wanted Ivan to go with them.

"I left less than a year after we parted company. I've been in Seattle all these years, teaching at the university. I haven't heard from you or Ivan in all this time. I didn't think there was a reason to keep in touch. I knew the time would come, but I didn't think that Ivan was going to pickle himself into uselessness," Kinsley explained.

"I hope we can sober him up. He's going to have to stay here until we shove off. It's going to be difficult to rehab him here," Tom said, adjusting Ivan's feet on the couch.

Tom put his arm around Jason. "Well, at least the captain is in sound mind, right?"

"As good as anyone else in this room. I can't believe we're going back. Things weren't so good when we left.

"Nara's brother was dissected and fed to the sharks. She is half-human. She was emotionally distraught over that finding. Having creature blood, she got over it quickly. All of that altered DNA that the sharks consumed caused them to mutate, also. Dr. Warren Wild has created a situation that is irreversible."

Jason went on, "Let's look to the positive thrust of our journey. Your grandchild will be the first water-breathing human to spawn generations to come that will survive global warming when the oceans reclaim the land. Jean and Pisces can live with you. You will be able to raise the child along with Jean and Pisces. As far as the sharks, we will get through. There will be two boats. Dr. Houcheck and his crew will be following us."

Nara sighed. "All right, then. Jason, why don't you stay with us until we leave? You can help Ivan withdraw. You can use the pool. It will be good for you…for us all. You can both share the guest house out back."

"I was hoping you would ask. My lease is up on my apartment. I intended to move anyway, but this way, I can take my time looking around. I'll stay with Ivan in the guest house, work with him and keep an eye on him. Thank you, both."

Tom went to the safe and got out the detailed report and video discs that they had completed after the discovery of the rogue and the colony.

"Good job, Jason. Good job," Tom commented as the DVD came to a close.

Ivan was snoring and drooling on the couch, having turned to his side.

"He'll be okay," said Nara. "Once he has something exciting to concentrate on, he won't miss the booze."

Tom yawned. "Tomorrow morning is time enough to get started plotting our course. Houcheck said that we only have to get to the colony. He and his crew will rendezvous with us there, and then the science team will handle Jean."

Chapter 11

Keenan and Shelby were packed and ready to board their direct flight to the coast. Rossano and Houcheck were going to meet them on the plane.

As they found their seats and put away their overhead carry-ons, they said hello to Rossano and Houcheck. They were behind them, in the back of the plane. Keenan squirmed in his seat and was dismayed that his knees were almost to his chin. There was little room to spare. He was hoping that sleep would keep him until they landed. Shelby got out a book and opened it to page one. It was a murder mystery. After what had happened to certain people who posed threats she decided to look over the notes of the trip, instead.

Keenan had his I-pod in his ears, listening to classical music to drown out the firing of the jet engines. He shut his eyes and tried to get comfortable. She had the window seat and enjoyed watching the take-off. The plane shook and moved forward, taxiing in a circle, turning around and zooming down the runway and up, into the air. Houcheck conversed with Rossano. They were comparing maps and data, each one oblivious to the flight, itself.

Rossano pointed to a place on a map and looked into Houcheck's face. "The sharks from Conch Island migrated in pursuit to Lake Danger. They mutated because they were eating DNA-altered flesh of the new conch colony creatures. We don't know how many there are now and how difficult it will be to pull our boats ashore."

Houcheck answered, "We have harpoons and explosives with us. When Moss called, he requested deep water mines be brought."

"Regarding the girl, Jean, I hope Micklos is gentle with her when it's time for sedation. She's very bright. I wonder if she picks up that she is the star of our show, or should I say, the baby is. Do we know if it is a girl or a boy?"

Houcheck grinned. "I believe it will be twins. No tests have been done yet. She didn't want to know the sex of the child...old-fashioned, you know. Not very scientific. It has been the trend in this strain of DNA that there always twins...girl and boy."

"She is in for many shocks, poor thing. What a honeymoon!" Rossano laughed. "My own honeymoon was over very shortly after my marriage. It was annulled. She wanted to 'save herself' for marriage, but it turned out that she was frigid. I think she was after my inheritance. I don't trust any woman, anymore."

"You are better off without them, Mark. Believe me. I couldn't have achieved all that I have done if I had a wife and or children to consider. You are a young man. Who is to say that you can't satisfy your male urges and not get entangled in a permanent relationship?" Houcheck laughed.

Rossano responded with, "I guess you are right. I just had an ideal in mind when I proposed. Perhaps I was too young, too trusting. We all have something to contend with. Right now, I will concentrate on the grand project."

They both looked out the window into the clouds. It would be a long flight. Keenan was asleep and Shelby stared out the window, in a daze. Her data file was on her lap, never opened. She didn't mind flying, but hated the inconvenience of being checked in at the airport.

Jean was upset about the disappearance of Dana, her close friend. Now, the police were involved in a search for her and Mark Zabor, another friend of hers, who could not be located. She made her plans to fly away to her honeymoon at the new colony on Lake Danger. What an adventure it was to be, discovering a place that no one but her husband and his parents had seen.

The nuptials arrived in Parchment Prairie. The desert house and the glistening pool were a welcoming sight in the hot afternoon sun.

Three days later, they would embark. She met Ivan and Jason for the first time.

They pulled up and unloaded their luggage. Jean stopped on the way to the front door and called Dana again. This time she got an answer. Her heart jumped. Nothing was wrong, she thought. "Hello." It sounded like Dana.

"Dana! Where have you been?" Jean shrieked.

"It's me. Ann. We haven't found her yet. The police are really trying to find her. They wanted to talk to you, too, but I told them you were newly married and on your honeymoon. I doubt you know any more than we do here, but don't worry. Hey, you are on your honeymoon. You are not supposed to be worried about anything. You and your handsome groom are on your way to a great time."

Jean sighed. "Ann, you sound so much like your sister. I was excited for a minute. I am still worried, but am hoping that her crazy brain has schemed a tryst with Mark, who I never thought was involved with her. They are really not chemically compatible."

"You never know, Jean. We'll see. Just enjoy yourself. I will text you about what happens. Joy to you and your new family."

"Bye, Ann. Thanks." She folded the cell phone as Pisces watched, waiting for her to join him at the door.

Nara was waiting with Tom, and a third person looked over their shoulders. She wondered which one of the crew it was. It was Jason Kinsley. Ivan was resting in the guest house. He was withdrawing from alcohol and being quite irritable. She would meet him later, at dinner.

The door opened, and Nara put her arms around the both of them. Tom and Jason wet back into the living room.

"Jason, this is Jean, our special daughter-in-law, mother of our first grandchild."

Jase put out his hand and shook it, saying, "It's a real pleasure to see this cowboy find himself a beautiful cowgirl. Congratulations! He is a real gem." He winked at her.

"I'm glad to meet you, too, Jason. You must tell me more about where we are going. Tom, I mean Pisces, doesn't tell me much. He just says, 'wait and see.'"

Jason nodded without saying anything else.

Jean asked, "Where is Ivan? Isn't he staying here, too?"

Pisces put down the suitcases, and Tom helped him drag them down the hall to their room.

Nara said, "Ah, he's resting in the guest house. The sun bothers him sometimes, but he'll be all right. He'll come out eventually. Drink?"

"Do you have any iced tea or lemonade? I'm on the wagon until Junior or Missy is born."

"Sure. Sit down. I'll be right back." She went to get drinks.

"How was your flight?" Jason sat down in a chair near the picture window. He adjusted the blinds to direct the sunlight upwards.

"Uneventful, thank Heaven," said Jean, sitting down on the couch. "I'm always waiting for someone to stand up, flashing a gun around, shooting innocent passengers, and blowing himself up in the name of Allah. You know, nothing is safe anymore."

Nara returned to the living room. She set the tray down on the coffee table.

Down the hall, Tom asked Pisces if Jean was okay. He told his father that she was fine, and that she wasn't suspicious of anything.

"Good. Maybe she will surprise us when she realizes what is in store," said Kinsley. "So, Pisces, how do you feel about spawning the first perfect hybrid to kick-start a new generation of water-breathers on the entire planet?"

"I'm happy about it. I am a part of it, and so is Mom. It's all I have heard about from you guys, and I want to see this place and meet Dr. Von Horst."

"Great. I am the outsider. I am 100% Homo-Erectus. I can't even conceive of the enormity of this conversation. Let's go."

They walked back through the dark hallway into the brightness of the living room. Nara walked to the kitchen to look out the back window. The guest house was small, but furnished very well with air-conditioning, large flat screen TV, WIFI, and all the modern conveniences. It had two separate rooms for each of the team members. Ivan was still sacked out on his bed. Soon enough he would become hungry and walk over to the main house. Nara shook her head. She hoped the sobering process would be over the time they left.

She was preparing something different for dinner. There would be a turkey with all of the trimmings. A Thanksgiving feast was to be had before they left as a symbol of what was to become the gift of the world. Let the global warming ensue. Let the polar ice caps melt, let the oceans swell and flood the land. Soon, all of Humanity would be able to survive under water. It made her feel warm in her heart that she was a part of it all. Her real mother was unknown to her. She only knew Professor Horace Nordic as her biological father. He was a hybrid, her mother was human. Nara felt special and important, plus she was happy with her human husband, content to live out her life with him in the desert till death do them part.

Jason was in deep conversation with Jean when Tom and Pisces entered the room. Jean looked up when he walked over to her.

"Jason is fascinating, I would like to talk longer, but I am so tired. Do you mind if I take a small nap before dinner?"

"By all means, please, get some rest," said Jason. Pisces stepped back to let her walk to their room.

"I'll see you all later." She disappeared down the hall.

Pisces and his dad sat on the couch. "You got lucky, kid. She's a keeper." Jason settled back in his chair. "I wonder how Ivan is doing. I guess he's sleeping instead of drinking. There is no alcohol at the guest house. He must be behaving."

After dressing the turkey, Nara put it in the oven. She had made dishes and had them ready to heat, covered with tin foil. There was a cake in the refrigerator for their glorious celebratory dessert. The writing on it said, "Happy Honeymoon and More, Jean and Pisces." There was an icing image of The Ocean Glory in a wake of blue frosting.

"Is Jean all right?" Nara turned her head, looking down the hall.

"She's okay, Mom. She's just really tired. I told her to rest until dinner." He patted the seat next to him on the couch. "Sit down. Relax. You're working too hard."

She flopped down next to him. "I wish we were going along with you. I am so curious. You will get to see our grandchild before we do."

Tom said, "You're more human than I thought, Grandma. I'm not that anxious to be called Grandpa." He laughed. "Let's take this opportunity to go over the plans." He pulled out the books from under the couch. They gathered around. "Ivan can catch up tomorrow. He's got to be fresh in the morning."

Chapter 12

SHELBY, KEENAN, HOUCHECK, AND ROSSANO met at the baggage claim and waited for a limo to take them to the hotel. It was early afternoon. They would spend the night there and hit the marina very early in the morning. Keenan had bags under is eyes from sleeping so long.

"I'm getting coffee. Any of you want some?" he asked. He looked at his watch.

The others passed. Shelby wanted some, but didn't want to take the time to drink it. She just wanted to shower and dress for a dinner in a nice restaurant in downtown Seattle. Every now and then she thought of Dana and how she appeared to have just vanished. And, Micklos, who was supposed to meet them at the marina, said that Mark was gone without a trace, too. The head of the lab assistants, who went overseas to be with his sick mother, never returned. She hoped that none of the detectives were smart enough to connect the dots.

They checked into a Holiday Inn. Micklos was sitting in the lobby wearing dark glasses. He watched them walk in. They didn't see him until he stood and said in a loud voice, "Over here."

Shelby pointed to him, and they walked over to him. Houcheck said he would catch up, but wanted to get the keys to their rooms. He was eager to go over the plans before morning. Micklos waved at him. Houcheck nodded and continued on to the reception desk.

"Micklos, glad you're here. You must join us for dinner. We're eating in the hotel. We can all meet in Houcheck's room later. Are you ready for tomorrow?" Keenan shook his hand, heartily.

Micklos towered over all of them. He was dressed in black, his bald head gleaming. He was a fine specimen of Russian muscle. He showed his teeth in a wide smile which was something he didn't do often. Shelby had to remember that he was a killer, chosen by Houcheck to cover the tracks and keep their project safe, until such time as they could reveal it to the world.

Chapter 13

The day was coming to a close on the desert where the Latimers resided. Lara was swimming nude in their pool. Tom was reading in a reclining chair. She winnowed beneath the surface and rested on the bottom, smiling and waving up to him. He took a short break from his reading, which was a rehash of their original trip to Lake Danger, including pictures of the queen conch and Dr. Von Horst. He came across a picture of her father, Horace Nordic. How did he ever attract any female and get her to agree to lay an egg, even if it was for science? There was no picture of her mother. She was the only child of two very prominent scientists. She tried to contact her, but she faded into oblivion after the colony was destroyed off Conch Island.

He shuddered when he remembered how quickly he hooked up with Nara. Of course, Nara knew that an egg was fertilized when they had intercourse in the pool, but he didn't know that she was going to lay an egg. She did. Things turned out all right. He did love her, and their son was going to carry the torch by having a child with Jean. It bothered him that Jean didn't know what was going on, but he was an innocent, too. He wondered where he would be if he hadn't met Nara. He had nothing going for him, otherwise.

Nara came over to him, dripping wet. "Are you going for a swim?" she asked.

"No. I'm kind of tired. I might lay on the couch for a while in front of the TV and wait for a call from Jason. I am expecting him to let us know how they are doing."

Nara put on her towel and walked inside. It was cool and dark in the living room. She walked to the kitchen to pour some tall iced teas. Tom followed her, carrying his paperwork. He flopped down on the flowered sofa and turned on the television with the remote control.

All parties traveling up the Darlington to the rogue to the hybrid colony had gone over the plan three times before turning in early. The first to wake up was Jean. The sun wasn't up yet. She didn't sleep very well. It might have been her midday nap, or it might be that she was uneasy inside about everything. Hormones might have been playing havoc with her emotional state. She quietly left Pisces's side and walked to the window to watch the sun come up. There was a slight red glow on the horizon. The purple mountains were turning red. Black pines were turning dark green. The gray sand brightened.

Jean stretched and yawned. She looked over at Pisces whose eyes were open. He had just wakened.

"Good morning," he said.

"Good morning. I'm so ready to go. So far, I feel good…no nausea."

"Well, that's wonderful." He sat up, pushed off his covers, and walked toward her. "Let's wake the others. It's almost time for the rooster to crow. I think we should push off no later than seven."

They heard Tom's voice, then Nara's. Someone came in the front door. It was Jason and Ivan. They were trying to keep their voices down, but noises carried in a one-floor home.

Pisces called out, "We're all awake now. See you in a few minutes."

They dressed quickly and moved to the living room. The sun was spreading across the prairie. There was some cloud cover that might or might not dissipate.

"Hey," said Ivan. He approached Jean. His face looked pasty. He wasn't a bad looking man, just aging fast. He extended his hand to her. "Am I pleased to meet you, Jean! Sorry I was AWOL yesterday. I never did wake up till it was too late to come over. Missed dinner and everything. I'm starving."

Nara appeared in jean shorts and a halter top with sandals. "I set the coffee maker to go off at six." The rooster crowed and the chickens began fussing and clucking in the barnyard. The light went red on the coffee maker. "Voila!"

Tom said, "Eggs all around, toast, and sausage. I'll help. You guys just go over the van and make sure that we have what's on the check list." He began getting out breakfast food. Jean put her personal bag next to the door. The pool was glittering under patchy blue sky.

Keenan, Shelby, Micklos, Houcheck, and Rossano sat at a big round table in the hotel restaurant. They had served themselves at the buffet and were on their second cups of coffee.

Houcheck paid the bill. Their SUV was packed and ready to go.

"It's a beautiful day to start our journey. I think, from what Tom told me, it will take until late afternoon and then, we should tie up and wait until morning to navigate through the barrier of vines to Lake Danger."

Shelby wore white light-weight pants and canvas white shoes. Her blouse was also white, worn over a white tank top. Keenan was in khakis as were the others. They left through glass doors and got into the vehicle.

Keenan set the GPS to find the marina. It would be about an hour's drive from Seattle.

Houcheck belched. "Anyone have any Tums? I think I ate too much, too fast."

Shelby handed back a bottle of them from her place in the front seat. "Here. Take four."

"Thanks, Doc. Anyone else have indigestion?" He passed the bottle around. No one else took any. He gave it back to Shelby.

They traveled along highways to smaller roads that led to a sparse landscape of dirt, tumbleweeds, and small bushes. Mountains loomed in the distance.

"There is a road that runs next to the river. It shouldn't be far," said Rossano, following the map with his finger.

"Relax. The GPS is leading us. We're turning onto the road now. Wow! The Darlington is wider than I thought. "Follow the road 40 miles until you come to Mercury Boat Sales and Rentals," came the confident voice from the directional device.

The windows were open, and Shelby's hair was blowing around. Keenan put in a classical CD. Rossano, Houcheck, and Micklos were taking in the scenery from the back seat.

The other group was settling into the van. Jean pulled out her phone to text Ann again. Pisces gently took it from her. "No. Wait until she contacts you. She doesn't know anything yet. She's probably infatuated with that guy, Zabar, and they are off somewhere having a fling. You know how she is."

"But, maybe..."

"No, Jean. Please. Let's just be happy. She will let you know when she comes home." He gave her phone back. She put it in her pocket.

"She's going to hear it from me when she does. First, she misses my fitting, then a lunch date, then the wedding, itself. I would never do that to her."

"You are not her. Look, there goes an iguana. Look at him run. I bet the sand is hot." He pointed to the green lizard running crazily to the shelter and shade of a rock.

"How long till we get to the boat?" she asked.

Ivan answered, "About an hour."

Jason drove. Ivan rode shotgun, and Pisces and Jean were going to get in the back. Nara and Tom stood outside the van to say goodbye.

Jean put her bag in the car and hugged Nara first, then Tom. Pisces hugged his mother and shook his father's hand.

"We'll see you soon. Have a great time you two!" Nara called out as they got in.

They watched the team leave, knowing what was unknown to Jean. She had to be in the dark. No harm would come to her. She would return when the child was born, and it would be raised in a human world, spreading hybrid genes across the nation.

Ann was beside herself. She didn't want to call Jean, but the police were certain of foul play. They didn't know where Dana went that day, but she disappeared two days before Mark, so they didn't think the missing persons were just a couple off on a lark. They told Ann that her co-workers at the paper said she was working on a real hot story, but couldn't reveal it yet. She and Mark were pals. He worked there, too, as copy editor. Maybe they knew something that was not to be revealed. No one knew anything. As far as the lab technician that took her to the party at the Morgan's mountain retreat, he never came back. They were checking into his whereabouts, too.

Fermin Levine popped out the door of the shabby building that housed his office. He was wearing flip-flops, a sleeveless tee shirt, and a pair of olive drab Bermuda shorts. He was even balder now, almost twenty years later. He wore sun glasses and was chewing on the stub of a cigar.

"Hey, you guys! Your men were here working on the boat all week. Big trip planned, eh?" He greeted them on the gravel and shook their hands.

"I am Tom Latimer's son. This is my bride, Jean," said Pisces.

"I thought you were your father, but then again, how could you keep so young looking after these years, and be with another woman. Shame on me for thinking you had a second wife." He laughed. "You know, your mind starts to go when you get to be my age." He shook Jean's hand. "I remember you guys." He shook Ivan and Jason's hands. "We heard there was a resort upriver. It's totally new. It's our honeymoon, and since we have able-bodied navigators, we thought we would venture forth and explore."

"I haven't heard of it, but then, I don't keep current with most things. My eyes are blurry...cataracts that have to mature before I can see well again. I don't read much or even watch TV, but I don't want to hold you up. It might rain today. The river might swell. Have a great time! You can fill me in when you get back."

They boarded the boat, and Jason took his place at the helm, starting the engine, untying the ropes. It was loaded and ready to go. They pulled away from the dock as rain drops started to fall. The clouds covered the sun. The radio weather said intermittent showers, mostly sun. Pisces and Jean sat at the back of the boat on the padded bench seat, enjoying the passing scenery. Flowers were in bloom on the banks. River birds fed in shallow water.

The Morgans and the others that comprised their crew arrived about a half hour later. Fermin Levine, the marina owner, didn't have a clue that they were going to follow them to the rogue, and that it was visible for three days after the full moon. It was a forgotten lure, still. This would be totally new to them. It wouldn't be easy to play hide and seek on the water. Once they arrived, it would all make sense. Von Horst was eager to have them arrive. His health was holding, although he was weaker than when Nara laid her egg.

Jean lay back on the padding. Pisces noticed a slight bulge in her abdominal area. He put his hand on it.

"You are starting to show. That is exciting. It's beautiful." He gently ran his hand over it.

She looked at it from her prone position. "I guess I will be getting fat and ugly. I hope you don't lose interest in me." She smiled and shut her eyes against the sun.

"Never will I lose interest in you. Besides, looking like a mother-to-be is a beautiful thing. It means we are multiplying." He had a serious look on his face, as though he had said something poetically profound.

She laughed at the thought of multiplying, even though that's what was happening. He imagined cells under a microscope splitting in two, then four, and so on. He was embarrassed. "You know what I mean. I'm not so good at expressing myself."

"Of course I know what you mean. And now we are three." He chuckled and gave her a kiss.

Kinsley gave the wheel to Ivan, who was sober and serious. He gave him a bottle of water instead of his usual flask. He guzzled it and asked for another. Kinsley pushed the cooler up close to him and pointed to it. "Help yourself, bro. Keep on course. We've got a ways to go until we come to the old kayak rental place and remember that weird crooked tree trunk."

Kinsley sat on a deck chair, pulled his hat down over his eyes and napped, feet on the deck table. Pisces and Jean rested in the sun.

Micklos was the navigator on the other boat. It was a yacht of good size, but it was definitely the economy model. No real leather or fancy doodads, and the necessary bathroom was small. Sleeping quarters were like shoe boxes. It was called "Catfish". He towered over the wheel. He was wearing khaki shorts and a white fishnet top. His bald head was red and shiny.

"Put a hat on that thing, comrade. We don't want you to fry your brain." Rossano's white teeth showed in a smile as he handed Micklos a baseball cap.

The big man snatched it and placed it roughly on his pate. He put on some speed and skirted out of the marina onto the river. It had stopped raining, and the clouds were gone. The temperature soared. Houcheck and Rossano sat at the table. Shelby and Keenan leaned on the side railing, feeling the spray of their wake on their faces.

Houcheck said, "I'd like to catch up to The Ocean Glory after dark, so we can watch when they set sail and keep close surveillance with binoculars."

Rossano said, "Hey you two, watch out for sunburn. It is quite hot on the water."

They cruised around boulders and tree branches. There must have been a storm, recently. They passed the white boulder to the left, near the bank. It looked like a dinosaur bone.

"We should take a sample of that," said Houcheck.

"It's not important. Most likely, calcium from something upriver, like fleshy discard from the hybrid experiments on the rogue," answered Rossano.

Jean sat up, looked around, and lay back down. Pisces was standing at the railing, watching the water go by. He thought that Jean was asleep under her big straw hat. It was fastened under her chin, so it wouldn't blow away. He took the opportunity to go below and swim in the cold water tank. It was his form of exercise. Once in the room, he shut the door and stripped then, climbed the ladder and fell backwards into the cold water. The tank was about eight feet deep, and the water was clear.

Ivan continued to steer around rocks and debris as the river narrowed and traveled around a bend. There were birds gathered on a sand beach as he skimmed over the current. Jean opened her eyes, wakening from her short nap and looked for Pisces. She guessed he went below and shut her eyes again, but remained awake.

Jason got out of his deck chair and stepped up next to Ivan. "I'll take over, if you want a break."

Ivan turned to him, face showing traces of sunburn. "Sure, I could go for some shuteye." He turned the wheel over to Jase and took his place in the deck chair, taking with him a large bottle of cold water.

He looked over at Jean. He thought she was sleeping. He shut his eyes and dozed off.

Jean got up and went below decks to see where her husband had gone. He wasn't in the cabin or the bathroom. The door that was closed was the only one left. She opened it into the tank room and saw him asleep in the corner of the tank, on the bottom. She knew he could hold his breath for long periods of time, but he looked dead.

She knocked on the glass, where he rested in a fetal position. She became frightened and climbed the ladder. Ivan walked in and called out to her, "Jean, he's all right. Get down from that ladder. It's dangerous for you to be climbing like that. He's all right. I know him well enough to know that he is just resting. He is breathing. It's his phenomenal ability to breathe underwater."

"What?" she asked, breathless as she backed down the ladder?

He gently pushed her back and went up the ladder himself, jumping into the water with his clothes on. He sunk to the bottom and reached Pisces, who stirred from his nap from the disturbance in the water. Ivan touched his shoulder and pointed to Jean, who was standing outside the tank. He quickly shot to the surface and broke through the water, not gasping for breath, managing to maintain even breath. Ivan surfaced, quite out of breath.

When Pisces's head popped up, he said, "Jean, honey, I'm all right. I'm not dead. I told you I can breathe underwater. I'm sorry I scared you." He pulled himself onto the ladder and descended. He was naked. She handed him his shorts and shirt.

Ivan pulled himself out after him, clothes heavy with water. He sloshed down the rungs and stood beside them. Pisces was climbing into his shorts, commando. He pulled his shirt over his head and hugged Jean to his cold, damp body. His hair was plastered on his forehead. Ivan looked weary and wet.

"We've left Jason topside by himself. I suggest we join him. We're getting close to where we have to identify our bearings," said Ivan.

Pisces kissed Jean, and they climbed the steps to the upper deck, where Jason was looking around to see where everyone had gone. When he saw them emerging from below decks, he maneuvered the yacht into the shade near the bank, stalled the engine, and dropped anchor.

"We need a break for lunch. I'm starving," he said. "What were all of you doing down there? Swimming?"

"I needed to hydrate," said Pisces. "Jean thought I was dead at the bottom of the tank. I was just taking a short snooze." Pisces hugged her to him.

"Weird, isn't it, Jean? Who would believe that we have Aqua Man in our midst," said Kinsley, making his way back to the others.

She sighed. "It's a little hard to get used to, but I love him," she answered.

Ivan commented, "Just wait till you give birth to a tadpole."

Pisces frowned. "Don't listen to him. He's an old drunk."

Ivan stepped forward and got into Pisces's face. "I wouldn't bring that up, if I were you, punk. We all have things we hide and are ashamed of. At least I'm trying to change my ways." He sneered at Pisces.

He backed away from Ivan, realizing that he was a ticking time-bomb and had to be handled with kid gloves. He didn't want him bringing up the real reason they were traveling the rogue to Lake Danger and the colony. He had to keep him and Jase from letting plan details be leaked. He had to keep Jean calm and interested in the workings of the colony and meeting Von Horst and his associates.

The Ocean Glory cruised along, around the bend to the kayak rental which was no more. Just a few boards remained, indicating there was once a building. The white twisted tree trunk remained. Jason showed the boat down and got closer to the bank to be sure. "I'm guessing this is the spot, after all, it has been twenty years."

Let's keep going, and everyone keep a sharp lookout for the opening where the grass is marshy and seems to flow left of the main stream," said Ivan.

They traveled on for a long, boring stint. There were a lot of large rocks on either side of the main channel, not to mention the occasional hidden rock, dead ahead. The boat hit one, and Ivan, who was then at the wheel, turned sharply to avoid damage.

"Slow down," shouted Jason. He went up to the helm and took the wheel from him.

"I am. I am. I didn't see that rock. We're going to have to go slow for a while," Ivan answered.

Pisces and Jean joined them. "It's treacherous here. Look ahead... rapids. Take her over them easy. They don't look too bad, but the rocks are all around," said Pisces.

Jean held onto the rail. The boat was bobbing up and down as it neared the white water. "How far are we from the rogue," she asked.

Jason shouted over the din of the rough water, "Not far, Jean. As I remember, when we get to the bottom of the rapids, there will be a large, swampy area to the left. We have to maneuver our way through the mire and through the circle of bamboo that leads to the silver lake...Lake Danger. You'll see. Hold on."

The Ocean Glory's bottom was getting battered, but she held her own. Jason was a good skipper. The craft glided over the rough, white water. Everyone was getting wet. Finally, after taking a curve, the water became calm. On the left, a light green patch of marsh grass appeared. It led to a tangle of vines and heavy brush.

Pisces pointed to it. "There it is. We found it," he shouted. He put his arm around Jean. "We have to anchor and spend the night. It is too late to undertake breaking through. Anchor upriver, Jason."

Jason shut off the engine and dragged the anchor. The boat undulated in its own wake near the bank. The sun was heading for the horizon. It was late afternoon.

Ivan was gulping down bottles of water, wishing they were vodka. He didn't feel well. He should have been left behind. Jason, Jean, and Pisces hugged each other and jumped up and down.

"We need to go over how we're going to do this. Last time we were here, we had to use poles to push the boat through," Jason explained.

Rain began to softly fall on the deck and dimple the river. Clouds moved in and blotted out the setting sun.

"I don't feel very well. I'm going to lie down," said Jean to Pisces.

With a look of concern on his face, he said, "I'm taking my wife below decks to settle her in the bunk. I'll be back. Don't start without me." He escorted her down to their cabin and kissed her as he covered her supine body. "I won't be too long. If there is anything I can get you, let me know. I'll be right in the den."

"Okay. I'm fine, really. I just need to rest."

He shut the door to the cabin and walked into the circular living room area with a round coffee table and padded chairs surrounding it. Maps and coffee cups were on the surface of the table. He took a seat along with Ivan and Jason.

"Is everything all right with Jean?" asked Jason.

"Yeah, yeah. She's just tired. It's due to her condition. Let's plan tomorrow. I hope the rain clears up by then. I say we begin no later than six."

They nodded and began discussing their plans.

On the other boat, the Morgans, Rossano, and Houcheck huddled around their table to discuss their plans. Micklos was already asleep in his cabin. There was no need to include him until they got there.

"Once they have cleared the way, it shouldn't be hard for us to get closer. Six o'clock should do it. Let's turn in," said Houcheck, the head honcho.

"According to speculations regarding Jean's pregnancy, there might be an advancement of growth. In other words, she might have this child or children much earlier than a normal term birth. I am glad Keenan and I can deliver her." Shelby yawned. "I'm going to bed now. Come on, Keenan. Goodnight, gentlemen. See you in the morning."

They went to their cabins. Houcheck and Rossano hung back a while to finish some details that remained unclear.

Soon, the boats were rocking gently, and all parties were fast asleep.

Chapter 14

At the colony on Lake Danger, rains drummed on the thatched roof buildings that housed tanks of experimental conch hybrids.

Heinrich Von Horst massaged his heart in the privacy of his room. There came a knock. It was Barrett.

"Come in." He pulled his vest over his ailing heart and carried on as if it weren't bothering him.

"I wanted to see you before tomorrow. We can do nothing about the sharks. They are bringing explosives and mines to drop after they come ashore. Until then, the sharks will be fierce when they come through the channel from the Darlington."

"Don't worry. It will work out. We can throw them some chum from the failed experiments. We will toss it to the far end of the lake when we know that they are coming through. It will give them a head start," said Von Horst.

"Fine. Then, I'm turning in. Moss is already asleep."

"Good. You get some sleep now, too. I was going to go to bed before you knocked."

Bed chambers had been readied for the crews. Moss had placed a bunch of flowers in a crystal vase in Pisces's room as a honeymoon surprise. It would be the only thing that would cheer Jean up. On the day of arrival, she would be subject to tests and have to meet the others.

On board The Morning Glory, Pisces lay down next to Jean, trying not to wake her. She was awake anyway, staring at the ceiling, feeling her abdomen. She turned to him and said, "Feel it. It's much bigger, now."

He put his hand on her belly and was amazed at the growth in just one day. He pulled the covers down to get a better look.

"My God, Jean, I can't believe it! Why the growth spurt?"

"I don't know, I've never been pregnant before. Do you think it's that strange?" She sat up and put on a cabin light.

"I think I saw movement. Do you feel anything inside?" Pisces also sat up, his eyes wide.

"I have been feeling fluttering since this morning. I'm going to have to wear one of your shirts. I don't think I can button my jeans. I didn't account for gaining weight around my middle to fast."

"Okay. Let's get some rest. He shut off the light. When we get to the colony, there will be doctors to check out what's happening." They both lay down and went back to sleep.

Ivan said to Jason before turning in, "Did you see how big Jean's bump is? It wasn't like that when she boarded the ship. I think it's odd." He headed to his cabin.

Jason commented, "This is an experiment. Things will be different. It is the perfect hybrid she is carrying. Maybe she was given growth hormone. We'll see when we get there. Dr. Morgan will check her out. See you in the morning."

Ivan looked over his shoulder. Jason stopped at the bathroom before going to his cabin. He pulled his door shut and opened his duffle bag. At the bottom was a bottle of vodka. He smiled in the dark as he unscrewed the lid. He drank from the bottle, sitting on the edge of his bunk and consumed the entire fifth. Sleep came easy after that. His body crumpled over, dropping the bottle to the floor.

Jason had been watching Ivan for days, keeping him from drinking, observing his behavior. He seemed stable, but he should have known that this trip would reinstate the old, irresistible craving. He thought he heard a noise from the cabin when the bottle hit the ground, but was too tired to check it out.

Chapter 15

THE MORNING BROUGHT A DRIZZLE, and a thick fog covered the river. It was six o'clock. All hands on both decks were making coffee and getting ready to continue on their way to Lake Danger. The bright green reeds of the marsh were undulating from the divergent river current. Sounds were those of early birds and waves slapping against the boats.

On the second boat, Catfish, the doctors Morgan, Houcheck, Rossano, and Micklos were on deck, conferring.

"Cold Pop Tarts for all!" Houcheck held up his and took a hearty bite. "No more cooking. These will fuel us just fine."

"Nutrition can be in the form of a breakfast treat," said Keenan. "Filling our stomachs is what is important this morning. I think the sun is going to burn this soup off in about an hour. Let's get ready to launch. We are not far behind the others. Once we can see the channel in the reeds, we will follow them."

Pisces, Jean, and Jason were on deck with their coffees getting ready to penetrate the tough entranceway on the rogue to the lake. There was a damp chill in the morning air before the sun fully rose. Pisces put his arm around his wife. Did he imagine it, or was her bump even bigger this morning? He was alarmed, but didn't mention it to her.

"It's exciting, isn't it? We are almost there," she said, shivering.

"We are fortunate to be involved," said Pisces, being careful not to mention what was about to happen."

Jason approached. He was tending to the ropes and swabbing the deck.

He asked, "Did either of you see Ivan? He's usually up at this hour. I better go below and check." He went downstairs to Ivan's cabin and knocked on the door. "Ivan! Are you up?" He rattled the doorknob. It was locked. He heard Ivan stirring, moaning, and a thud as Ivan fell out of bed, hitting his head on the table next to it. He groaned, loudly.

"Open the door! Get up! We're all waiting for you. Today is the big day, remember? You are not sick, are you?"

Ivan was groggy. He felt his head. There was a small gash that was bleeding. He got to his feet and stumbled to the door. He slowly opened it. He was shaky and baggy-eyed.

Jason could tell right away that he had been drinking. He saw the empty vodka bottle next to the bunk. Ivan started to crumple. Hitting his head seemed to stun him even more than the hangover.

"I can't believe it!" said Jase. "It was too good to be true that you could kick the habit in so short a time. Let me see that cut on your head." He assisted him to the bunk and sat him down. "I'll bandage it for you. Then, you've got to wash up and get topside. I'll have coffee waiting for you. I want to keep your condition from the others." He got clean clothes out for him and put them on the bed, next to him.

Ivan had his eyes shut as he tried to lean back and return to sleep.

"Oh, no you don't. Come on." He marched him into the small bathroom and ran a cold washcloth over his face and neck. Ivan revived and pushed him away.

"All right, all right, I'm okay now. I'll be fine. Leave me be. I'll join you in a minute. Let me get dressed for Christ sake." He stood straight and ran a comb through his gray, tasseled hair. The flesh-colored bandage wasn't too conspicuous.

"I'm counting on you, Isaacs. We're in this together. This is huge. Don't let us or yourself down." This being said, Jason left to go upstairs.

He passed the galley. Jean was getting more coffee for herself and Pisces.

"I take it you found Ivan," she said.

"Yes, I did. He was just slow getting ready. He'll be up in a minute. Any more of those scrumptious Pop Tarts?"

"We have quite a few boxes. Here, which ones do you like best?" She held out three boxes with assorted flavors. He took the box of chocolate with sprinkles.

"These will do. See you upstairs on deck."

He joined Pisces, who was looking through the binoculars into the fog.

"I can see nothing, but the fog is lifting."

Jean emerged from below with the mugs of steaming Joe.

"It's getting warmer, like a steam bath. We should rub down with insecticide. I have a feeling the mosquitoes and flies will be swarming in the swamp."

"Good idea. I'll get it." He went below and bumped into Ivan who was on his way up. He smelled of soap and hair tonic. His clothes were clean, and he didn't stink of booze. No one would know, except Jason.

"Morning, son." He kept walking past Pisces to the top.

On the Catfish, Micklos was restless. His big frame leaned over the side as he looked into the opaque fog.

"We got up early for nothing. I am still tired. And so, we wait." He spoke in a Russian accent. He seemed disgusted with life most of the time.

Shelby answered him. "It's a good thing we are up early. What lies ahead is going to take all of our concentration. We don't know what is on the other side of this rogue connection."

Rossano said, "Let's get our ammo ready in case we encounter those hybrid sharks that Barrett talked about. He said to bring explosives. We have plenty. We all have a weapon, too. We've got to be ready and expect anything."

Houcheck turned to them. "All will turn out well. I trust each one of you to perform your duties as planned. Sharks, or no sharks, we will carry out the plan." He drank his coffee and grinned.

Jean smoothed Pisces's long white shirt over her abdomen. She jumped and turned to Pisces. "It's kicking! It feels like a lot of arms and legs moving, trying to beat its way out."

Pisces felt her stomach. His face showed concern. "You should have had them do a gender test. We can't even name it until it is born. It sure has a lot of energy. How are you feeling? Still sick in the morning?"

"No. I really feel quite strong. This is peculiar, though, having something actually growing inside you. I have all respect for motherhood now. I have no idea when the due date is. Maybe it will be born here, God forbid." She laughed, not knowing that she spoke the truth. God forbid!

Ivan overheard the conversation and was watching them from aft. He began laughing and holding his sides, loudly breaking the semi-silence of a misty morning on the water.

"What's gotten into you, Ivan? Did we say something funny?" Pisces was hoping that he wouldn't hint about the near future at the colony.

"No. I was just laughing, thinking that there are sharks in this water. I don't see any, do you? They are all crazy in that colony... bunch of hybrid-maniacs." He slipped and fell to the deck on a puddle of rain water.

Jason pulled him up. "Are you all right? We're pushing off soon. The mist has almost risen, and the sun is beating down. Get up and see if you are okay."

Ivan brushed himself off and rubbed his shoulder. "It will be all right, Captain. Let's shove off and visit that colony of misfits." He imitated Humphrey Bogart and laughed.

No one else laughed at his antics. Jason said, "I'm taking first shift at the helm. All of you be ready to assist when the going gets rough. There are bamboo poles on deck and rifles that are loaded in case you need them. We've heard there are sharks. Crazy as it sounds, we better be ready."

The boat powered in closer to the bright yellow-green area of swamp reeds. It plowed through them until the engine caught on underwater weeds. Smoke spiraled out from behind her, and the smell of diesel permeated the atmosphere.

"Shut her down, Jase. She's stuck already. God! What a hellish mess this is," shouted Ivan, sweating, craving another drink.

Pisces stripped down to his shorts and moved to the rail in the back. Jason cut the engine. The smoke dissipated. "I'm going down to free the rotors. You know I can hold my breath. It's not a problem for me. Just don't start the engine, right?"

Jean grabbed his arm. "But, you don't know what's down there. Maybe there are sharks."

He gently unloosened her grip. "I'll be back before you know it. Give me that machete. Keep the pole handy, too, so if I need it, you can hand it to me."

She handed him the big knife for hacking and stood, ready with the bamboo pole. He slipped into the marshy water over the side. Quickly, he submerged under the boat. They felt him cutting away the confining plants. To Jean, it took forever. Ivan and Jason knew well that he was able to do this after witnessing Nara do the same thing on their maiden voyage.

Jean was very nervous.

"Don't worry. He's our hero. Wait and see," said Ivan.

A few more bumps from the underside and Pisces's head popped out of the water. His breathing was as even when he got out of the water as it was when he jumped in.

"I cleared away a lot of the junk down there. I think we can make some headway. Turn on the motor, Jase." He put on his shirt. His hair was plastered to his forehead. Jean hugged him and put her head on his chest.

"I hope you don't have to do that again."

"I might have to do a lot more than that. I can handle it. I told you. You just observe and enjoy the adventure of the trip."

The long, river weeds closed in on them. The vegetation was getting denser. Not much of the water was showing. It was as though they had almost gone aground. Bang! The boat hit something hard, like a rock. Everyone was thrown to the ground. Jean was almost thrown over the rail. She gasped. She had studied water and oceanography, but was not a strong swimmer and did not like to be in it.

Her heart was beating fast, and the infant she carried was having spasms, it seemed. She experienced a great flutter of arms and legs, and then, the baby rolled over, throwing her off balance. She held onto Pisces, who had gotten to his feet, for balance.

Ivan stood and looked over the side. "What the hell was that?"

The front end of the boat rose, and the crew had to hold on to keep on their feet. The Ocean Glory moved forward fast with the help of something in the water that was under the boat.

Dear God, thought Pisces, I hope it's not a shark. What have I gotten into, Jean?

The boat lurched and went from side to side. As the waterway became more apparent, they saw what was creating the turbulence. It was a large, shiny white fish with a small fin that protruded upward, perpendicularly. It had mighty muscle and a big mouth full of needle-sharp teeth. Its eyes were large, black circles, bigger than those of common sharks. It was a hybrid. Mutation was caused from eating the flesh of mixed DNA in the conch colony. All discarded experiments were cast into the water. These sharks that had migrated in search of the flesh on Conch Island were not thriving in Lake Danger. Most hybrids and DNA crossbreeds were known to grow more rapidly and reproduce more frequently than normal creatures. Science was botching up nature just as fast with it meddling in God-given life forms.

Its broad head surfaced to the side of the boat with its wide mouth open. It was aiming for Jean, who had just slammed against the railing. Before Pisces could get to her, Ivan grabbed her hand and pulled her away from the menacing monster. In doing so, he slid across the wet floor and pitched over and into its mouth, screaming. Pisces dashed to his side and pulled his feet. His head and upper torso was sliding down the shark's gullet. Its jaws closed onto him and with blood gushing and muffled screams, sounding. The shark pulled away, going down into the water below the boat and even deeper into the swamp. Pisces was left holding the shaking legs and lower torso of Ivan. The rest of his body was gone. He was dead in seconds. No one could have saved him. Jean became hysterical. Jason accelerated the speed of the boat, and it moved forward, freely toward the bamboo circular gate that led to the silver waters of Lake Danger. A shocked

Pisces tossed the bottom half of Ivan over the rail into the bloody water and consoled Jean.

Jason called over his shoulder as they went through the open gate, onto Lake Danger. "Get the sedatives below decks. See that Jean takes a dose, and you, too. I'll be all right, for now."

The Ocean Glory was speeding toward the bank across the large silver lake. Von Horst, Barrett, and Moss were waving and smiling from the sand beach, unaware of the brutal murder of Ivan Isaacs by a hybrid shark. A line of swarthy natives from one of the Conch Islands, stood with rifles aimed at the water. They were watching for a shark attack, even though the chum had been cast to the far side, as a diversion.

Chapter 16

ABOARD THE CATFISH, HOUCHECK SAID, "We're just going to cruise slowly along until we get a glimpse of The Ocean Glory. Then, we will take cover until she clears a path for us."

He started the engine. Beads of rain water and splashes from the plants on the bank rolled off the Catfish's bow. Its blue finish matched the patches of blue forming in the sky. Clouds were breaking up quickly and drifting away. It was getting hot. Steam was rising on the water. The boat slowly began to move, following the bank until it came to the opening where The Ocean Glory had gained entry to Lake Danger. They bore left and started their trek inward on the rogue. Poles were in readiness should the Catfish get stuck. So far, they were free and clear to travel. Shortly after their turn in the swampy entrance, they noticed the water was tinged red. Keenan and Shelby scooped up a vile and tested it. They discovered that it was blood. What had happened? What could have caused this spillage? They were hesitant to believe that it was a shark doing damage.

"We better be very careful. It looks like something awful happened here in this passage," said Shelby.

Houcheck held up the test tube to the light. "It's blood all right, but whose?" He passed it to Rossano, who frowned and turned it around, examining the ruby color in the light.

Keenan took it from him and disappeared below decks to store the vial, quickly returning to join the others. The journey was getting exciting. They approached the bamboo gate and proceeded effortlessly through the portal. As they cruised onto the silver waters of Lake Danger, they saw The Ocean Glory, beached on the sand bank of the colony. They chugged forward, cautiously approaching. Those on shore looked out over the vast expanse of silver water, and Von Horst was the first to wave them in. Jean was the only one not expecting company. Micklos steered toward the landing spot and docked next to The Ocean Glory. He cut the engine and helped the others off onto land.

The small group met the larger group. They were introduced and shook hands all around. The Doctors Morgan were amazed at how far along Jean was. Houcheck's eyes bugged when he viewed her bump, knowing that it was twins, but still amazed at the speed of growth. Were they abnormally large, or just father advanced in the term? He made notes in a little book he withdrew from his pocket. His glasses were at the end of his nose. They had slid down from the intense humidity. The smell of sea flesh was all around them. Jean was nauseated by it.

"We are both doctors. This is my husband Keenan, and I am Shelby, his wife. We will tend to you while you are here. I think the first thing we should do is get you to an examining room and make you comfortable. She nudged Keenan, who was already giving orders to Von Horst to make a room ready.

Von Horst called Moss over and told him to lead them there, that it was ready for them.

Micklos stood like a huge statue, sullen expression on his face, cold eyes staring.

Pisces conversed with Barrett. He explained that the shark had eaten Ivan in the passage through the swamp. Barrett was worried. The sharks in the far corner of the lake, who were feeding on chum, got wind of the blood in the water and were frenzying in the middle, where the vortex used to be. Their short fins looked like silver blades, standing, erect in the glittering water. They were heading for the beach full speed ahead, sensing a feed.

The natives began shooting into the flotilla of hungry predators. Some of the bullets missed and splashed into the water. Others hit their mark, and some of the sharks leapt out of the water, wounded.

The others, crazed with their lust for blood and flesh, began to cannibalize their brothers. It was a massacre that slowed them down and diverted their intentions to raid the beach. There was thrashing and tearing of flesh, and the silver lake became red and violently disturbed.

Von Horst led the guests quickly into the bamboo dwelling, where the labs, offices, and tanks were housed. They looked over their shoulders as they hurried inside. The native army kept shooting. One strong shark made it to the beach, and to their shock, stepped onto the sand with webbed feet at the end of sturdy legs. Two legs pulled its huge body onto land, as it headed for the closest native. He turned his rifle on its head and fired four times. The animal had crawled almost to the pathway to the buildings. Blood shot everywhere. The other natives ran for their lives. Boolee was the bravest and best shot. He killed the beast, kicking its dead head with a bare foot, grinning, showing a mouthful of white teeth, with some missing.

"Good job, Boolee," shouted Von Horst over his shoulder as he entered the compound.

Inside the confines of the colony, the air became danker. There was even a mist on the ground, rising from the stone paved walkways. Little shells that held candles were fastened onto small supports along the halls. Jason was the only one who had been there before. Every now and then he remembered that Ivan was gone. He wished that Tom Latimer was along, too. Things had changed. There were more cages, more human-looking hybrids. None of them resembled Professor Nordic or the queen conch. Where was she?

He stepped up to Von Horst, who was more stooped and frailer looking than the last time he saw him.

"Where is the queen conch? I thought she would be very interested in witnessing a human birth, and one that carried her DNA."

He paused and sighed. "Unfortunately, she fell into the jaws of a walking shark. One of her babies wandered into the water. The shark was seen speeding to the beach, mouth open. She tried to scoop it up before it hit, but was too late. It snapped both of them apart, swallowing them in halves. They squealed, bringing out the natives, who witnessed the legs on the sharks for the first time. They were not only in shallow water, but could also crawl forward toward the compound. It was another mutation that occurred since the migration of island sharks arrived in Danger Lake."

Jason exclaimed, "Are we safe here? When you shoot at them, they frenzy from the blood in the water. How many are there?"

Von Horst held his chest as though a heart attack was coming on. "Get me my..." He fell over. The others following them managed to get Moss to administer his medication. Every time this happened now, Moss and Barrett thought it was the end of Dr. Von Horst. But, he revived. The natives brought a litter and carried him to his quarters. Shelby went with them. Keenan was getting Jean ready for her exam. Pisces pushed past them to be with Jean.

She was lying on a straw mat that cushioned a rough examining table. There was a woven blanket over her legs, knees were propped up to allow entry into her womb. Her abdomen was now a dome of some size. There was motion going on inside. Little knuckle images appeared and disappeared. A large shape, like a head or a buttocks, rolled over under the skin. Then, two shapes like grapefruits rolled over. Jean wondered what that could be. She hoped her child was normal.

Keenan inserted a few gloved fingers into her vagina and felt for the head. There were two. He thrust his hand in further and found that there were two bodies, each having two arms and two legs. He did not know the sex from this type of exam, but Houcheck said they were female. The infants seemed healthy and ready to be born very soon. He was amazed at the speed of their development.

After withdrawing his hand from her private parts, he said, "You have two healthy babies, almost ready for delivery. How do you feel?"

"Twins? I didn't think I would have them so fast. It's only been a few months, and I am afraid of this high-speed pregnancy. Why is this happening? How many times do pregnancies go this way? I have never heard of it before."

He helped her sit up, and she pulled down her long shirt to cover herself.

"Dr. Morgan..."

"I can't explain it, Jean, but everything looks fine. You can stay here and deliver them, re-cooperate, and leave when you are all strong enough, as a family, to travel back home." He patted her knee and assisted her off the table. She was shaky.

"What about these sharks? Can we safely navigate our way back to the Darlington? We lost Ivan. In saving my life, he fell into the jaws of a monster." She shivered, remembering.

"I can't lie to you. We are trying to eliminate the sharks, but we have to blast them with dynamite, mines, grenades, and harpoons. Our native troops are ready and very skilled in this process. We have to get you settled in here, first. At night, we carefully watch the sharks as they will come up onto the beach and walk on two sturdy legs up to the entrance of the colony. If you hear shots, know that you are being protected from them."

"Oh, I wish I had stayed behind. This is supposed to be our honeymoon. It is very disappointing. I don't feel at all secure giving birth here. There is so much danger around us." She shuddered.

"That's why we call it Danger Lake. But, you won't have to stay more than a month after the birth." He smiled, like there was nothing wrong.

"Can I be air-lifted out of here?"

"No."

"Why not?"

"This is top secret, this colony here. Are you familiar with Warren Wild's theory, of returning man to the sea so that Humanity can survive Global Warming."

"Is this what it's all about? Of course, I have heard of it, but I thought that the Conch Island colony failed. I thought that this was just an experiment to see why it failed, not to build a new one."

"It's already functioning on the back side of the bay that is not visible. It is a fresh-water colony underwater of water and air-breathing hybrid conchs with human DNA. I will show you the creatures that are used for testing. They are in tanks and cages in the laboratory. You will find it fascinating."

"I want to find Pisces first and tell him the news that we are having twins. He will be stunned. I guess that explains all of the continuous motion inside me. I am eager to have them in my arms."

"We are all happy for you and wish to see the new arrivals. Don't fret over anything. Dr. Von Horst will provide your every want and safety while you are here. Shelby and I will be with you during delivery." He continued smiling, again, like nothing was wrong.

He ushered her out into the hall to where the creatures were kept. In that room, there was a screen that video-taped all activity underwater on the back side of the bay. She gasped when she saw what the hybrids looked like. They were big, fattish, white, and shiny, like slugs. They had black eyes, like polka-dots. Their arms and legs were thick with webbed toes and fingers. There were many of them eating crawfish whole and raw and going in and out of a building made of white coral-like material, most likely, calcified stone. Small fish swam by in schools. It was dark under the water. Long, undulating river weeds camouflaged the entrance. Inside the door, she could see real conch shells that stood about three feet tall. Cradled in these were white eggs, laid by the conch creatures. The sharks could not get to the colony. It was too narrow and protected by big rocks below.

Pisces had been meeting with Von Horst, Barrett, Moss, and the others: Rossano, Shelby, Keenan, and Houcheck. They crowded around a table in a primitive conference room. They had discussed the birth, the treatment of Jean, when she discovered what part she was playing in the plan, and the fact that Pisces was involved in hoodwinking her into becoming pregnant. He knew about the twins, but would act surprised.

The meeting adjourned. Pisces joined Jean and Keenan in the laboratory.

"Pisces! We're having twins! Can you believe it?" Jean approached her husband.

"You're kidding!" He hugged her tightly and kissed her on the forehead. "That's wonderful! Boys or girls?" He already knew that they were daughters.

"I still don't want to know. Does it matter? We'll love them anyway."

Shelby walked into the room, overhearing what Jean just said. "You have great will power. If I had children, I would have been dying to know. Congratulations! Twice the joy." She hugged Jean. Of course, they all had a special interest in the issuance of perfect hybrids.

Chapter 17

Tom Latimer crossed the living room with his cell phone in hand. Nara was on the sofa, watching the news.

"It's Pisces. They've arrived and are going through orientation. They lost Ivan to a shark."

Nara gasped. "Oh, no! They must be multiplying. Poor Ivan."

He spoke into the phone, "Twins? You have got to be kidding! How is Jean? Does she know about them yet, boys or girls?"

Nara's ears perked up at "twins". She got up and stood next to Tom, pulling the phone to her ear to share in the conversation.

She spoke to Pisces. "Why don't you know the sex of the babies?"

"Jean doesn't want to know. She is so old-fashioned. It really doesn't matter, does it?"

"Yes, sir. It certainly does. I am going to be decorating the room for them. I am going to be the doting, although too young, grandmother."

"Listen, I've got to go. All is well so far, except for our casualty with Ivan. Dr. Von Horst is not well. He's aged, considerably, but I have to go now. Next time we see you, we will have our babies in tow. Bye now. I'll call again when I get a chance."

Tom closed up the phone. "Things are happening so fast. I can't wait until things are restored to normal around her. Drink?" He walked to the bar.

"Sure. I need one."

Ann was calling the police again, as she did every day. The officers on the desk were sick of her inquiries. They had no clues. It was becoming a cold case. She refrained from texting Jean when there was nothing new to tell her.

The monitors in the lab and in the office showed the far portion of the lake, where the sharks were diverted with experimental waste flesh. They were busily fighting and frenzying over the white seafood substance. Another camera took videos of the beach, where an occasional shark wandered into the shallows and attempted to climb onto the sand with its two sturdy legs. They were immediately shot by native guns. This game went on all day, whereas the diverted numbers sensed the blood in the water and headed to the beach to cannibalize any shark that was shot.

The final views were of the entranceway, the office, and the sleeping chambers. The back doorway entered into the back colony, in the reeds.

Shelby quickly re-appeared in the dining room, just as coffee was being served.

"Dr. Houcheck, everyone, Jean is not in false labor. The twins are about to be born. It's astounding that they are here so early, but they are both normal size and healthy. From what we have gathered, gestation is only three months instead of nine. I have to get back. Keenan and I will deliver them. We will keep you posted. Pisces, come with me. Hurry!"

Dr. Houcheck stood, also. "I must be there to see this. I'm coming, too. Kinsley, Barrett, Moss, and Rossano, you stay here and finish your coffee. Micklos, see if you can help the native army fight off the sharks."

The big man stood and walked out towards the beach, where the natives were taking pot shots at the sharks, who were approaching the beach, in semi-darkness.

Micklos took grenades and mines with him. He also had a flame-thrower to deter them.

Chapter 18

Jean was prepped for the delivery. She had been given a shot as the infants seemed to be in a hurry to be born. Her forehead was wet with beads of perspiration. She twisted and turned, trying to get comfortable. Pisces was at her side, holding her hand, kissing her now and then, reassuring her.

The doctors Morgan were monitoring and feeling inside her for the head of the first one.

"Everything is normal, Mommy. Relax. It's not time yet to push. Hold on," said Shelby. "I know it's going to feel like your back is breaking. It's normal; it will pass. Your contractions are getting stronger. It only means that the infants are getting in position to travel down the birth canal. The pain will subside, I promise. One of them is lined up and, oops, your water just broke. That's good. It won't be long. For your first babies, you are doing very well. You can push now."

Houcheck stood behind the doctors, but was able to witness the emergence of the twins.

"Things couldn't be more perfect. Good job, Jean. Good job!"

Pisces said, "Hang on, honey. I'm here for you. You're doing a great job."

In spite of the shot she received, Jean screamed as she pushed like her insides were turning out.

Pisces was nervous, not wanting to see his wife in pain. Soon, they would know if the experiment had worked. He would have to tell Jean. They would have to stay to have tests done on the babies before returning to Latimer's desert house to start normal lives. He was counting on maternal instinct to cover the shock of having water-breathing hybrids for children.

"Ahh!" she screamed so loud, he swore the walls shook. She dug her fingernails into this hand and drew blood. Tears sprang from her eyes. She was exhausted from pushing.

He wiped her brow and gave her a cloth to chew on. The contractions were coming in spasms. She pushed so hard, she almost went off the end of the table. Shelby had latex gloves on, waiting for the head of the first baby to crown. It was there. A black spot that became bigger, pushing the labia back, like rubber. Jean twisted and screamed again in agony. Pisces held her hands in his.

"Ahh...oh, God!" She yelled, thrashing around on the table.

"Hold her steady, Pisces. The first one is crowning, and soon it will be slipping out. Be ready to hold it."

He held Jean still. She tried to push him away. He fought to keep her still. Then, a baby cried, loudly. Keenan's hands pulled out the child. "It's a girl," he cried. He held her up. She was a beautiful, well-formed human baby. Houcheck beamed.

Jean burst into tears of joy at the sight of her. She tried to raise herself up on one elbow. Pisces pushed her gently back. "Hold on, babe. In just a few minutes you can see her. You have another one inside, remember?"

"Here it comes!" she screamed. "Ahh..." She moaned and twisted. Houcheck held the first, swaddled infant in his arms.

Keenan took a look under the tent made of sheet and saw the head of the second one crowning.

"Push, Jean. Do it one more time. It's coming fast."

Jean gave an enormous thrust from her pelvis, and the second baby emerged, crying. They both had light brown hair and were both female. He held up the second identical twin so all could see.

Jean went limp. Pisces applied a cold cloth to her forehead. She came around with smelling salts that Shelby held under Jean's nose.

"It's over, Jean. You have two beautiful little girls. We're going to do an episiotomy and clean you up you and the girls and get you settled, cozy and comfy. I'm going to get you a cup of tea, too. You need to hydrate so you can successfully breast feed."

Jean grabbed her hand. "Thank you." Her hair was spread out across the pillow.

Once settled in the primitive nursery, where two woven bassinets awaited the newly born, Jean said to Pisces, "I didn't think much of the anesthesia. I am so sore. I don't think I ever want to go through that again. Sorry. This is it...our final family count."

Pisces picked up one of the little ones that was wrapped in a pink blanket and handed to Jean. He picked up the other one that was crying and rocked it to sleep.

"Do you have any names yet? It's not important right away. We can wait until tomorrow, even. I'll let you nurse them first. Boy, are they hungry!"

"Help me. Put one on each breast, so I can feed them both at once. I don't want to have to do one and then the other. I don't even know how to do..."

Shelby stepped into the room. "I'll show you. It's a little tricky the first time. Pisces, will you leave us to our privacy, please. It should take about twenty minutes. Oh, they look so cute. They are truly beautiful, and they are identical."

Pisces left the room, saying, "I will be right back, sweetheart. You are such a good mother already." He blew her a kiss.

Shelby adjusted each newborn to a nipple. Each greedily foraged for a dripping teat. She assisted the infants by placing the nipple in each mouth. They screamed and squalled, even though the milk was flowing. Jean's breasts were swollen full with nourishment. One of them even spat it out and made a hideous face. Their tiny hands had fingernails that actually could scratch Jean's flesh.

"Stop! Get them off of me. They are hurting me!" yelled Jean, which set each infant into deafening cries of fear. They cried as though their hearts were breaking.

Jean was overwhelmed. She had expected a wonderful bonding experience with them. She was totally tired and not prepared for this outburst.

Shelby frowned. "Keenan! Come here!"

He rounded the corner with Pisces on his heels.

"What's wrong," he asked.

"Take the babies to the nursery. Jean needs her rest. I think they will be better off on formula." She whispered, "We need to dry up the milk. They are opposed to the breast milk."

Keenan nodded and took the infants from Jean, who was groggy and irritable.

"We will bring them back after you have slept a while. Don't worry about a thing. You can feed them when we bring them back."

Clive entered the room with a hypodermic behind his back. He slowly approached Jean, who was now appearing to be napping. He pushed up her sleeve quickly and injected a substance that would dry up her milk. She didn't stir. He then brought out another needle and inserted it into her other arm, shooting a heavy-duty tranquilizer into her vein.

"Good, Clive. Now she will rest and we can proceed. I want a formula made for these two. Make it full of seafood powder and greens. They can't tolerate human milk. We can keep her sedated now, without interfering with her lactation." Shelby pulled Jean's sheet up ad turned out the light. I'm sure Pisces will want to see his children. They are beautiful...a handful, but beautiful."

She pulled the door shut as they left Jean's room.

Keenan had the two babies in his arms as he walked down the hall. They were kicking and wailing.

"Shel, I'm glad we had no children. I don't miss this."

"You might be right. Maybe they won't be cuddly, like humans. It won't be easy to mother babies that reject love."

Pisces met them in the hallway. "Don't tell me that are crying. What's wrong? Jean was so eager to nurse them."

"It will be all right. They seem to want something other than mother's milk. They rejected the breasts. We will work up a satisfactory formula for them," said Shelby.

A voice called out from Von Horst's room. "Hey! Let me see those beauties. I can't believe we have done it. Bring them here."

Von Horst swung into a wheelchair from his spot on the bed. He wheeled himself to the door. His eyes were barely open from the sedative, and his face was sagging with age and wrinkles. Dark bags were under his eyes, but he was grinning when he saw them.

Keenan kicked the door open and walked in. The infants had quieted down and were cooing. One was sucking madly on her knuckles. They could already see. They were growing fast outside the womb, too.

Von Horst put out his arms. "Give me one."

Keenan lowered the swaddled baby into his arms.

"Be careful," said Pisces, taking the other in his arms. "Look at the curls, like mine. Yet, the faces look like Jean. How beautiful." He rocked the child and kissed its soft cheeks.

"Their skin is so white! Like pearl," said Shelby.

Von Horst held the one up to the light and let its arms and legs dangle. "Tomorrow, we introduce them to the water and prove that they can breathe indefinitely under the surface. This is all I want. Then, Pisces, you and your little family are free to go. Remo Moss is our staff psychiatrist. He will work with Jean to get her to accept what has transpired. Your lives will be normal after you return home. The girls will be home-schooled, like you.

Shelby took the baby from Von Horst and said, "Enough for now for all of you. You must get more rest, and the infants must feed." They turned to leave. "Goodnight, Dieter."

They walked down the hall to the nursery. Clive had a formula heated and ready to go. "One for each, Dr. Morgan. Let's hope they like it."

There were two rockers in readiness for the feeding event. "Pisces, you take one, I'll take the other. It's hard to tell them apart."

Each of them sat with a swaddled infant. Each infant accepted the warm seafood concoction that Clive had formulated.

Pisces said, looking down into the little face that sucked hard on the rubber nipple, causing bubbles to form in the bottle, "I'm naming this one Aquabelle." She cooed and gurgled while she consumed her warm liquid.

Keenan said, "What if they don't pass the tests? Won't that be a strange name for a little girl?"

"They will. I am sure of it. And her sister will be called Hydra. There. If Jean wants other names, she can choose them. I am hoping that she comes around, and that they love their mother, not turn away from her."

The bottle was empty already. Little Aqua was asleep with formula running down the corner of her mouth. She burped, without being burped. She was physically advanced.

He put her down in a crib on her stomach and covered her. With an adoring look, he and did the same thing with the other one, sitting in the rocking chair. She was a little fussier, but ended up finishing her bottle, too, and falling asleep."

"You better get your rest, son. They won't sleep long," said Clive. "You need your wits about you when you explain all of this to Jean. Right now, she's out like a light."

Pisces yawned. Shelby and Keenan yawned, and finally, Clive yawned.

"You've started something. I think we all have to turn in. Where are Micklos and Jason?"

Moss came running down the hallway. "Those Goddamn sharks with the legs are creeping up the beach. A couple of them made it to the door. They put their teeth marks on the wood. I hope the noise doesn't wake the babies. In a minute they will be detonating the mines and throwing grenades. Did you hear all the shooting?"

"No. The twins have been screaming," said Pisces, who had since put Hydra into her crib.

"Where are Boolee and his men? Are Micklos and Jason all right?"

"Yes. The beach is covered with blood. Boolee and his men are hosing it off and pushing the dead bodies into the water. The other sharks are cannibalizing their carcasses. Torches have been lit, so you can see what's going on, and the security monitors should be showing current activity."

All screens were showing the beach, covered with blood and pieces of shark flesh.

"Let's do these tests now. We don't have much time," said Houcheck. "I want to evacuate the team here on The Ocean Glory. The Catfish has been destroyed in the melee with the sharks. Go prepare Von Horst. We can take him to the hospital when we return. He will receive much better treatment there." He ordered Rossano and Barrett to take care of that detail.

Pisces brought in the twins, who were fussing and waking from their sleep. "Let's test them in the water before feeding. They will do better on empty stomachs."

Shelby took one, unwrapped the blanket and stripped the infant of its undershirt and diaper. It cried and flapped its arms and legs. It had grown about an inch overnight. Its eyes focused on Shelby. "Into the warm water, baby." Shelby stepped onto a platform that would put her level with the water. "Pisces, get in the water with Hydra before I let go of Aqua."

He took the other baby and stepped onto the platform that rose automatically and put them level with the surface of the water.

"Wheel in Von Horst. I want him to see this," said Keenan.

Rossano and Barrett escorted him into the tank room. He was listing to one side in the wheel chair, but he was cognizant. He nodded and grinned, raising his hand that made the peace symbol with two fingers.

Pisces jiggled the baby in his arms to quiet her. He said, "Kinsley and Micklos are outside tending to security. Boolee and his men are with them. All is quiet." The video monitor showed them cleaning up the beach. The fins were in the far corner. There were considerably less of them in view, but they still had to escape.

Moss ran down the hall after Jean who was heading for the tank room. She was staggering like a drunk, under the influence of a heavy sedative. Moss had tried to hypnotize her into believing that she knew all along that she was to be the mother of the new Humanity. She rounded the corner of the doorway and witnessed her husband on the platform holding one of the girls with Selby holding the other twin.

"Here we go!" Pisces plunged into the water, tightly holding onto Hydra.

"Stop!" screamed Jean, falling against the door jamb. Keenan restrained her. Moss came in, consoling her.

Hydra broke loose from his grip and swam to the bottom. She was breathing water, no holding her breath. She rolled into a ball and flexed her arms and legs, sitting on the bottom and lying prone, only to shoot up and grab her father's leg. He was descending effortlessly. He pulled her up to his shoulder, looking like a religious painting of Christ with a cherub. She smiled and pushed away from him, performing stunts in the water, like a fish.

Shelby released Aqua, who was squalling and kicking into the warm water. She immediately swam to the bottom to join her twin in a water ballet. Pisces stood in the middle, on the bottom. They climbed him like a tree and put their arms around his neck.

Chapter 19

J ASON BURST INTO THE TANK room. His clothing was ripped and bloody. "We have to leave now. Micklos and the others are setting fuses to blow up the mass of sharks. Barrett, we could use your help. Start gathering all of the gear to load on The Ocean Glory. Someone get Von Horst ready. We are leaving the colony. We don't need the subjects anymore.

Houcheck interjected, "But they are our physical evidence of..."

"Sorry, Doc, we need to split now! You've got what you want – the perfect third generation twin female water-breathers." Kinsley picked up some supplies from the ante room and headed to the front door to clear the beach and rendezvous with Boolee and Micklos.

Jean was confused. "Wait, wait! Why are you talking about my babies like they are part of an experiment? Pisces, what is going on? I demand to know!" She walked to the crib and picked up one of the babies that was chewing on its fist. "She's hungry. I need to feed her." She opened her blouse, but her breasts had shrunk to normal size and were dry. "My milk is gone!" The baby that she held was Hydra. Her little hands pushed Jean's breast away and wailed, while its little body wriggled.

"Jean," began Shelby, taking the baby from her arms, "it's just that they are special. Now, let's get ready to leave and go home. Would you like that?"

Jean went to the other crib and looked at the other twin, Aquabelle, who was sucking her thumb.

"Keenan," said Shelby, "get the prepared formula and let Jean feed one of them while we all pack it up."

He warmed up two bottles and handed one to Jean. She sat in the chair and satisfactorily fed Hydra. It put a smile on her face. "There, there, little one. Mommy is here. Mommy loves you."

Pisces said, "I have named them Hydra and Aquabelle. I thought you would like them."

Jean looked up at him, frowning. Then, after a few moments, she nodded. They are good names. I will give them their middle names. They can use either when they grow up."

Jason burst into the room and started barking orders and pushing everyone toward the front door.

"Everyone has to exit immediately. Get onto The Ocean Glory and don't stop to gather anything. We are going to blow this whole compound up. The sharks are winning, and we are becoming weakened by this futile battle."

Pisces took one twin, Jean, the other. The doctors Morgan followed them. Barrett came in behind Kinsley.

"Hurry! We can't hold them any longer. They will be on the beach soon. Go! Go! Go!"

Moss and Rossano got Von Horst by carrying him by his feet and under his arms. Houcheck was checking out the video surveillance screens.

"Houcheck! Move it!" Kinsley grabbed him by his narrow shoulders.

"They are going to destroy the colony! What about the conchs and the hybrids behind the compound?"

Kinsley gritted his teeth. "They are going to die. Do you read me? Get going!"

More water poured into the lab. There was another explosion. Water gushed in white forceful waves into the lab and down the hallways. Kinsley braced Pisces and his family, sheltering them from the water with his arms and pushing them into the force to get out the door. The infants were wailing. There were distant explosions where the grenades were being thrown. The Ocean Glory rocked violently in its mooring. Kinsley pushed Pisces and his family towards the boat, across the blood-soaked beach. It smelled of burnt flesh and gun powder. The heavy fish oil stunk.

Kelsey managed to get them up the ladder, onto the yacht. It was rough going, but they wound up below decks in the salon where they could at least sit down and wait for the launching.

"Sit tight. Pisces, stay with Jean. I'm getting Shelby and Keenan next, then Von Horst." He was wild-eyed and out of breath, but thinking fast on his feet.

Micklos was heaving grenades and Boolee and Barrett were running fuses from the cache of explosives to the compound and around the far side of the lake. Rossano and Houcheck fled from the compound, carrying supplies and tripping up the ladder onto the yacht. It was like a war outside. The silver water was rough from the agitation of the sharks thrashing and the bombs going off underwater. The vortex became activated and it looked like a huge drain hole in the middle of the lake. Monster hybrid sharks were whirling around, caught in the whirlpool that led to an underground holding tank beneath the compound. The water was bloody. Some of the animals were ripped and dying, others were tearing at their flesh and flipping violently as they whirled downward, disappearing to the depths of Lake Danger.

Von Horst was being wheeled to the yacht. He was half out of the chair as Keenan pushed it top speed toward the yacht. Shelby helped Boolee push a cart of supplies to the boat.

Micklos was single-handedly commanding the natives to go downstairs and check what was happening below from the whirlpool. They ran, shouting and waving their arms in the air.

There was a howling noise that was deafening coming from behind the compound in the colony.

Kelsey was almost ready to light the fuse, but had to open the hatch to warm up the engine so it wouldn't explode at launch. He worked fast, sweating profusely, bleeding on his arms and legs from injuries gotten from fighting the sharks and planting fuses. The engines began. All parties were on board, waiting for the last minute all clear to detonate the underwater bombs. Pisces, Jean, and the twins huddled together as the boat pitched forward. Von Horst, who had not moved since they boarded, sat in the wheelchair, his head drooped forward onto his chest. He was an odd color. He was dead, but no one noticed right away. There were more important things to tend to, like a perfect escape.

Shelby turned to talk to Keenan, finding him not there with the others. "Where is my husband?" she screamed over the noise. She rose and was cast to the ground by the vibrations. She hit her head hard on a sharp edge.

On shore, Micklos, Keenan, and Boolee monitored the beach, taking the perfect placement and opportunity to light the fuses and jump to safety on The Ocean Glory that had been flushed out of the lake into the channel that led to the gateway, through the swamp and onto the Darlington River proper. The entire boat was lifted on a wave caused by the explosions and propelled over the channel onto the river current. Luckily, it cleared the rocks that studded the banks.

It slapped down hard and took off toward the bend. Kelsey and Barrett managed the wheel. It was rough steering under those conditions, but The Ocean Glory rode the turbulence and slowed to a normal speed once underway on the main current.

Micklos, Keenan, Boolee, and his men were all blown to bits, not making the jump to the ladder as the boat took off. No one could see what was left behind, only speculate. The entire compound was in flames. Sharks walked in the whirlpool tanks, but were boiled to death by the fire against the glass. Some sharks were thrown into the trees, caught on branches, or even impaled. If any of the shark hybrids survived, there would be no food source, since the hybrid conchs were destroyed, never to reproduce again. All evidence of the research started by Warren Wild, passed on to Von Horst, and finally finished by Dr. Houcheck, was destroyed. The experiment was a success. Two females would start the chain of reproduction that would alter Humanity and save it from the sea when global warming would melt all ice caps and flood the earth.

Chapter 20

Ann took a call from the police detective, who was working on the missing person's report of her sister, Dana.

"Yes, this is Ann," she said.

"This is Detective Franklin, ma'am. We have new evidence in the case of your missing sister. We are not sure how it all fits in, but the cleaning lady found an appointment card under the desk that had Dana's name on it. It was for the same day she went missing."

"Appointment for what? Who was she supposed to see?"

"Doctor Shelby Morgan." He waited for her response.

"Dr. Morgan? I know my sister. She wasn't sick. I know that she attended a party with a man who worked as a lab assistant with Dr. Shelby Morgan and her husband, Dr. Keenan Morgan. They were working on a project of some kind. When I asked her what it was, she said it was a secret." Ann thought a minute, reflecting back on how her sister was a reporter trying to break into the newspaper with a big article. She had told her about the mystery of it. Her boyfriend might have known about it, too, but he disappeared also on a different day, so the two of them weren't together as suspected."

He told her that she had been very helpful.

"We have more checking to do, more leads, but thank you. We will get back to you. If you think of anything else, let us know."

At the precinct Detective Franklin asked questions of the two Hazmat men that ran the incinerator in the basement of the laboratory.

"Joe was supposed to leave early that day. When we got there, the furnace had already burned up a load of materials that needed to be cleanly destroyed. That incinerator even turns bones to powder. There's nothing left when it is done. Well, we never saw Joe, just figured that he did his job and left for the weekend."

Franklin said, "We checked with Joe. He didn't go to work at all that day. He quit, as a matter of fact, so he didn't run the incinerator at all. Someone else did. Thanks, that's all. You can go."

"But who…"

"Just go now. It's all right."

He walked out, scratching his head then, turned back. "Oh, we did see both doctors leaving the building when we started. They were working even though the building was closed, but they never disposed of anything. That was our job."

Detective Franklin went to Mark Zabar's apartment to look for clues. He found a picture of Dana with the lab technician at the Morgan's party at their cabin. Everyone there were scientists. She wasn't supposed to be there, but had wheedled her way into being invited to overhear anything that might give her a big breakout story. He stuffed the photo in his shirt pocket. Mark's computer and phone were gone. There was no evidence of any story that he might have been working on with her. Someone broke in and stole the evidence and most likely kidnapped and killed him. There were no fingerprints. Micklos was a pro.

Franklin took a ride up to the mountain house belonging to the Morgan doctors. They were not home yet from their hellish journey. He poked around and found nothing in the cabin. He searched the car. Nothing. But, in the garage, he found the bag with the discarded, bloody clothing and Dana's purse. He took all of the evidence and carried it to his apartment to piece it all together. He was going to pin the murder of Dana on them, but the other case of Mark was by a different hand. His case was still a cold one, with no clues. All in all, he thought they were related. They were hiding a story that the world of science did not want out. He wondered what it was.

He couldn't trace their whereabouts. They were very secretive about their travelling plans. The boat was rented from Levine, in Washington State.

Pete Bogan, Franklin's partner called. A harbor master had reported a boat missing three days after Dana disappeared. It must have been stolen at night, because he never saw anyone on the docks that day. It was a small boat, tied up with about thirty other boats. He had no idea who it was or where they were going.

Franklin wanted the water dredged in the harbor area and beyond, heading out to sea. He had a hunch that the boat might have been sunk, and they would find incriminating evidence, if they could find the wreck and the body.

When Franklin questioned Arthur, the door man at the apartment belonging to the Morgans, he told them that he only saw Shelby. She told him that her husband was off on business. "I never saw her leave the building that night, nor have I seen her or her husband, Keenan, since. Come to think of it, it does seem strange."

Now, Detective Franklin was thinking that perhaps Shelby killed her husband, too.

He had the lab scrutinize the ashes in the incinerator. There was DNA belonging to Dana in the rubble. It was obvious that Shelby and Keenan were under suspicion of murder. They would continue to work on finding the kidnapper of Mark Zabar, figuring that that person was in cahoots with the Morgans.

What was the secret they were trying to cover up? He thought it was an illegal cloning operation or some kind of organ harvesting setup.

Ann tried to call Jean with the news that Dana was murdered, and that the doctors Morgan, were being looked at as potential killers. She couldn't get through on her call. Her phone was inactive.

Jean comforted the twins. After feeding them, she held them both on her lap. They fell into deep sleep.

Pisces and the others worked up a document swearing each of the party involved to secrecy. Each had to swear and sign it. Shelby was still in shock and mourning over the loss of her husband, Keenan. Houcheck was the only one who kept the research papers in their entirety. Von Horst had lived to see the results of the third generation hybrid conch that would double the chances of a water-breathing generation. It was the start of what was to come, the salvation of the human race.

Pisces, Jean, Hydra, and Aquabelle arrived home at the desert house. The Latimers embraced their granddaughters and new daughter-in-law. Jason was invited to stay in the guesthouse. He and Pisces worked at the cement factory, where their identities were safe. Nara still had more money than anyone would need from her inheritance. Jean was a stay-at-home mom, who schooled her girls with the help of veteran, Nara.

Houcheck, Rossano, Moss, and Barrett, along with the grieving widow, Dr. Shelby Morgan returned to New York to sink into anonymity and take up other pursuits until such time as the twins would reach maturity. With the growth hormone in place, they would reach puberty within eight to ten years.

Rossano escorted Shelby to her mountain cabin. He wanted to make sure that she was stable enough to resume working. Moss suggested that they transfer her to Parchment Prairie in Washington State, so that she could be the private physician to Hydra and Aquabelle. She knew their makeup, whereas it could be dangerous to invoke questions from a regular doctor.

A surveillance car reported they were home. Franklin and two squad cars arrived.

Franklin pulled his gun, ready for a fight. He knocked and showed his badge when the door opened. Rossano put up his hands and backed up. Shelby stood, dumbfounded behind him.

"You know why we're here Ma'am. You are under arrest for the murder of Dana Blackstone."

She backed up and fell into the couch, crying.

"Where is your husband, Keenan?" Franklin approached her and turned her to fasten the handcuffs.

"He's dead," she said, blubbering.

"Did you kill him, too?" he asked with no mercy. "No, no. He died in an explosion. That's all I can tell you. My husband killed Dana Blackstone. I was just an accomplice."

"Why did you kill her? What was your motive?"

Rossano got nervous. She could spill the beans about the plan.

"Can't you see that she is under great stress, Detective? Can't you question her later?" Rossano comforted Shelby.

Franklin kept jotting down notes. He looked up and asked Rossano, "Who are you, and how do you fit into this puzzle? Did you know the victim?"

"I am Rube Rossano, an associate, and I won't answer any of your questions until I talk to my lawyer. The same goes for Dr. Shelby."

Franklin said, "She can speak for herself."

"I won't answer any questions either until my lawyer is contacted," she said.

"Very well. Let's go. He helped Shelby off the couch. "Pete, cuff Rossano, too. He might try something funny."

They put them in the squad car and drove off with the other two cars following them down the steep driveway on their way back to the precinct.

Houcheck, Moss, and Barrett were laying low in New Jersey. Already they had disengaged from their associates. They resumed their research in an obscure laboratory in Newark. The team worked under the name of Solo Solar, supposedly doing research on solar panels. They were incommunicado with the Latimers and Kinsley; and of course, Shelby and Rossano.

"Look at the news. Rossano and Morgan are in jail now for the murders. Rossano might be released or be sentenced for a short time, for withholding information leading to the crime. I hope they keep their mouths shut about the plan. It's going to be tough explaining away the colony and the explosion that killed Micklos and Keenan. Moss and Houcheck exchanged glances.

Chapter 21

Aт тне desert house in parchment Prairie Nara and Tom adapted to their granddaughters. The pool was where the girls spent most of their time, growing rapidly and developing womanly figures. Being home-schooled, they didn't get to socialize enough to meet young boys. Of course, the object of their existence was to become impregnated and deliver water-breathing children. This was all covert. Prospective mates would be seduced by them and would become incorporated into the plan, like Jean and Tom. They were so far, having a normal life.

Eight years passed, and the twins were reaching puberty already. They attended pre-teen dances and were allowed to be promiscuous. Neither one came home announcing an accidental pregnancy.

Nara and Jean took them to see a gynecologist in Spokane. Tom went along, leaving Jase and Pisces to cover for him at work.

"Why do we have to do this, Mom? I don't want to be examined," whined Hydra.

"Especially internally. Yuck!" Aqua was also upset.

Nara said, "Every young girl gets and exam at this age. It's nothing horrible. It's not pleasant, but it has to be done."

"Why does Dad have to come along" I think it's an invasion of our privacy."

"I'm going to the hardware store to shop around. I won't even be there with you. Just do as your mother says, okay? Then, we'll go out to lunch in a fancy restaurant and maybe do some clothes shopping."

The girls replied in unison, "Okay."

Inside the modern Women's Health Center, Doctor Ruby Jalna, OB/GYN, opened the door into her office.

She was a beautiful East Indian woman dressed in a white lab coat. Her black hair was away from her face and was beyond shoulder length own her back. She was petite with little hands.

"How beautiful you are!" she exclaimed when she saw Hydra and Aqua, who each wore their hair differently, but were still identical, even in height.

They smiled. "Thank you," they said in unison.

At least it wouldn't be a man poking around inside them.

"Who wants to be first?" she asked, smiling. "I promise I won't hurt you, and I will be very quick!"

"I was born first," said Hydra, "so I will go first."

She disappeared into the examining room. Jean went in, too. Nara and Aqua stayed in the waiting room.

Jean wondered why the doctor was so quiet while feeling around inside her daughter. She frowned and removed her gloves.

"Is anything wrong, Doctor?" asked Jean.

"No, no. I want to check your other daughter, okay? You can go outside and wait in the office, Hydra. Your sister is next. You can tell her it was nothing, right?"

Jean thought that the doctor had a strange look on her face. She was worried, hoping that there was no cancer or cysts or other negative findings.

Hydra took a seat outside, and Aqua got up on the table. She watched Dr. Jalna grease a rubber glove. She squeezed her eyes shut tight.

"Open your legs. Let them fall to the sides, so that I can see what's going on." she gently pushed the girls legs further apart.

It's all right, Aqua. If your sister could do it, so can you," said Jean.

Aqua hated the invasion of privacy and the fact that her mother was there in the room, as a witness.

"Ah, very nice. Healthy tissue. Uh-huh. Okay, so you are finished already. You can get dressed and go out into the waiting room with your sister."

She hopped off the table and took a seat next to Hydra. Nara poked her head in the office. Dr. Jalna shook her head. She wanted to speak to Jean, alone.

Jean's expression was one of expectancy. "Well?

"Sit down, Mrs. Latimer."

Jean sat down opposite the desk. The doctor began, slowly.

"This is peculiar. There is nothing wrong with either one of your daughters. They are quite healthy, but the truth is, they have no reproductive organs, and it's not because they are only eight years old. They seem to be older than they are. It is quite strange. They will never have children, but I am sure they will find partners in their lives. There are no ovaries or uterus. Everything else is fine."

Jean fell back into her chair. "Oh, my God!" she exclaimed. "How can this be?"

"It is not the worst thing, Mrs. Latimer. If they desire children in their lives, they can use a surrogate. They will never have a menstrual period. Some girls would love that. I, myself, would like that?"

"What happens next? Do I tell them?"

"I would not tell them yet. When they ask about why they don't have their periods, you can tell them then. Why upset things now? You have to do nothing...no medicines or exercises. It's just the way they have been formed. Be thankful that there is nothing really wrong. There is no need to come back for a follow-up."

Jean stood. She shook Dr. Jalna's hand. "Thank you, Doctor. It was a pleasure meeting you."

Dr. Jalna bowed her head and said, "Namaste."

They were not to contact Houcheck, Rossano, or Dr. Shelby Morgan until a pregnancy was determined in either or both of the girls.

The experiments that evolved over a period of twenty years were a failure. Nature had a way of preventing man's interference.

In the car on the way back to the house, Hydra asked her mother, "Well, are we okay?"

"Fortunately, you are both healthy and normal, no problems. You don't have to go back again. It wasn't so bad, was it?" Jean drove. She picked Tom up at the hardware store. He was waiting out front, sitting on a high curb.

"Hey! How about a steak dinner at the Walla Walla Roundup?" He opened the back door and slid in next to the girls. They were hoping that he didn't ask them about their appointment. He didn't.

Nara sensed that Jean had a secret. Jean would reveal the findings to her later when the girls were in the pool.

Pisces jumped into the water with the twins. They had all kinds of tag games they played for hours underwater.

Jean and Nara called Jason at the guest house and asked if he could come over. They asked Tom to stick around. He sensed something was wrong.

The four of them sat around the dining room table, drinking beers.

"What's this about, Jean?" asked Tom.

"I'm going to blurt it out. The girls are sterile. They have no reproductive organs. They will never have children of their own. The genes will not be passed on. Humanity is not safe from global warming now. Luckily, they are healthy, it's just that they are unable to have children." Her eyes were wide.

Nara said, "Oh, no. All of these years researching and experimenting with conchs and hybrids. All of the water, the loss of lives. What will we do now? We have to contact Houcheck."

Jason shook his head. "Because of all of this, we lost Ivan, Keenan, Micklos, Boolee, and Barrett. And Von Horst died thinking that the plan was a success. At least, that's a good thing."

"Does Pisces know yet?" asked Tom.

"No. I don't even know if I should tell him. What's the difference?" Jean asked.

Nara said, "I'm going to call Houcheck and tell him. Then, we can all live our lives in peace. I'm glad they won't be monitored or studied. They are sweet girls. I think we all were spared."

Chapter 22

THE SCENE THAT THEY LEFT on Lake Danger was one of total devastation. A blue panel from the Catfish floated by the reeds. A heavy mist hovered over the distressed body of water. A very slow whirlpool whirled around and around, gathering all of the rotting shark flesh into its own gullet. The compound was no longer standing. Nothing but shredded wood remained. Decomposing skeletons of the natives and Micklos were on the beach. The bodies of Barrett and Keenan were nowhere to be found. The sharks had found the cages of the hybrid test subjects in the back, underwater, and had eaten them, or they were otherwise destroyed by the merciless explosive charges fired when the party escaped.

No traces. Failed experiment. Lives lost.

Jean found out about her friends, Dana and Mark. It would be hard to shake what had happened, that the good doctors, Morgan were murderers, but she did have two children, lovely girls. She had a good home and a good husband with no money worries. All of that was behind her now. The girls were planning to teach her how to swim.

Houchek was devastated by the news, but a good scientist never accepts no for an answer. He, Rossano, and Moss were going to reconstruct the experiment and start over on a distant, unclaimed island, where they could save the world from global warming in secret. This time, it would not fail.

Published books by J. N. Sadler

Big Town
After Big Town (Sequel to Big Town)
Seedling: Evil Hybrid
Drifter
The High Road
Shillings
Braun
Mountain House
The Conch Conversion (Trilogy)
The Darlington Rogue (2nd book in trilogy)
Global Warming: Water Babies (3rd book in trilogy)
Neon: The Other World
Caregiver
Tortue
Incident at Braxton Hollow
No Warning
Property Of...
The Moneyscope
The Man Inside
The Fix
Burning, Burning: The Perryville Disaster
Neighbors
The Garden Sphere
House Arrest
Knights

Lightning Source UK Ltd.
Milton Keynes UK
UKHW041838180221
379033UK00008B/559/J